INNOVATION THE EINSTEIN WAY

Virender Kapoor is a thinker, an educationist and an inspirational guru. An alumnus of IIT Bombay and the former director of a prestigious management institute under the Symbiosis umbrella, he is currently the founder-director, president and chief mentor of Management Institute for Leadership and Excellence (MILE), Pune. His books on emotional intelligence, leadership and self-help have been translated into several regional and foreign languages. To know more about him, log on to www.virenderkapoor.com or visit his Facebook page: Virender Kapoor. You can also follow him on Twitter @virenderkapoor or mail him at virenderkapoor21@yahoo.com

Other books in the series:

Leadership: The Gandhi Way

INNOVATION
THE EINSTEIN WAY

VIRENDER KAPOOR

RUPA

Published by
Rupa Publications India Pvt. Ltd 2015
7/16, Ansari Road, Daryaganj
New Delhi 110002

Sales centres:
Allahabad Bengaluru Chennai
Hyderabad Jaipur Kathmandu
Kolkata Mumbai

Copyright © Virender Kapoor 2015

The views and opinions expressed in this book are the author's own
and the facts are as reported by him, and the publishers
are not in any way liable for the same.

All rights reserved.
No part of this publication may be reproduced, transmitted,
or stored in a retrieval system, in any form or by any means,
electronic, mechanical, photocopying, recording or otherwise,
without the prior permission of the publisher.

ISBN: 978-81-291-3510-0

First impression 2015

10 9 8 7 6 5 4 3 2 1

The moral right of the author has been asserted.

Typeset in Adobe Garamond by SÜRYA, New Delhi
Printed at Thomson Press India Ltd, Faridabad

This book is sold subject to the condition that it shall not,
by way of trade or otherwise, be lent, resold, hired out, or otherwise
circulated, without the publisher's prior consent, in any form
of binding or cover other than that in which it is published.

CONTENTS

PREFACE   vii

PRELUDE   xi
The Life and Times of Albert Einstein

1. BE ALTRUISTIC AND A SOCIAL ACTIVIST   1
   Perform Philanthropic and Benevolent Acts

2. PRACTISE HUMILITY   12
   Be Humble Even After Achieving Success

3. SIMPLE LIVING, HIGH THINKING   21
   Simplify Your Life and Don't Chase Money

4. COLLABORATE   27
   Getting Along with People and Social Networking

5. AWAKEN YOUR IMAGINATION   34
   The Mind's Eye

6. NURTURE ALLIED TALENTS   52
   All Work and No Play Makes Jack a Dull Boy

CONTENTS

7. DEVELOP A SENSE OF HUMOUR — 59
   Laughter Is the Best Medicine

8. THINK SMART — 66
   Make Your Mind More Agile and Productive

9. ACCEPT FAILURES AND SETBACKS — 75
   Life Is Not a Bed of Roses

10. DISRUPTIVE THINKING — 81
    Practise Inventive Leadership

11. COURAGE OF CONVICTION — 91
    Belief, Integrity, Solidarity, Honesty

12. ADOPT THE PERSONA OF EINSTEIN — 102
    Develop a Charismatic Personality

EPILOGUE — 111
The Twenty-seventh Alphabet

PREFACE

Albert Einstein is probably one of the most intriguing personalities of the last century, who continues to occupy a position of respect, bordering on awe, in the hearts and minds of people, even sixty years after his death.

To most, he is an enigma of sorts; a man possessing immense intelligence, so much so that his name has become synonymous with intelligence itself. A majority of people are not even aware of his contributions to science and technology. They don't know why he is revered so much by the world community—scientific or otherwise—and is considered the god of science and invention.

Before writing this book, I must have asked more than a hundred people, from diverse backgrounds, a simple question, 'How much do you know about Einstein?' The answer didn't surprise me as most responded, with a shrug, 'Not much.' And when I asked the same people, 'Would you like to know more about him?' their answer, 'Oh, yes,' again didn't surprise me. This gave me the direction I was looking for—everybody knows of him but nobody really knows him!

It will not be wrong to say that most people relate the equation, $E=mc^2$, to Einstein and a majority of them also know that the theory of relativity (without knowing what this theory actually is) was his brainchild. Yet, he is an enigma and different people view him differently at different times. Knowing about his life is like peeping into a rotating kaleidoscope.

How did Einstein acquire such a cult status? What was so great about him? How intelligent was he and what was his contribution to mankind? These are some facts that every common man would like to know about this uncommon man. There are a number of misconceptions about Einstein. People believe that he was an eccentric geek, a loner. Some even think that he invented the atom bomb. But most of these notions are myths, and it is important to know the actual facts.

Einstein possessed qualities that made him a great inventor, scientist and a very popular figure.

This book will be of immense use to readers, regardless of their profession. They would not only get to know Einstein, but would also be able to interpret his abilities, passion, intelligence, and above all his motivation to do what he did throughout his life—invent with a spirit of dream and drive. It captures the essence of Einstein's creativity in such a way that people who read this 'three-dimensional biographical account' will be motivated to become creative in their respective fields, and those who have a scientific bent of mind will pursue serious research and foray into the world of invention.

As an author, it is also important for me to bring the 'not-so-obvious' into the public domain. People must learn from this frail man the importance of humour and wit. In fact, creating or even understanding humour requires a high level of intelligence, and Einstein had that in abundance. His ability to articulate in simple words is another important facet of intelligence that one can learn from him. I feel he was one of the few heavyweights who said, 'Imagination is more important than anything else.' He imagined first and created later. He visualized a phenomenon and then translated it into mathematical form, and that is how he was different from others. He spent all his life interpreting and understanding the universe to uncover the secret of our existence. He worked on a much larger canvas than any other scientist had ever worked on. No wonder he said, 'The most incomprehensible thing about the world is that it is comprehensible.' His imaginative powers were beyond the imagination of ordinary people and that is why he was an enigma for most.

PRELUDE

The Life and Times of Albert Einstein

'There is a tide in the affairs of men. Which, taken at flood, leads on to fortune; ...On such a full sea are we now afloat, And we must take the current when it serves, Or lose our ventures.'
—William Shakespeare

Early Life and Schooling

Albert Einstein was born in Ulm, a town in Germany, to a middle-class Jewish family on 14 March 1879. His father was a salesman and an engineer, who subsequently started a business of manufacturing electrical equipment.

He began his schooling in Munich, where he found the system to be very rigid that allowed no freedom to think or to be creative. As a student, Einstein was a rebel. He did not like rote learning and believed instead in self-study. Therefore, he bunked classes and earned a bad reputation in the eyes of his teachers. In his early days, he faced problems with his speech and spoke slowly, often waiting to decide upon his words.

Einstein developed a liking for music, as his mother encouraged him to learn to play the violin. He also learnt to play the piano. He became serious about music when he heard the compositions of Wolfgang Amadeus Mozart, whom he revered till the end of his life. Actually, his affair with music started at the age of thirteen, when he fell in love with the music created by Mozart.

After his father's business failed the family moved to Italy, leaving Einstein in Germany to continue his studies. Einstein disliked the way he was taught and soon left school to join his family in Italy. He later applied to a polytechnic school in Zurich, Switzerland. He didn't do well in the entrance exam, but scored very well in mathematics and physics.

His habit of curiosity had started taking shape at the early age of five. Even back then, when his father gifted him a magnetic compass, he wondered at the invisible forces that moved the compass needle. His imaginative mind developed when he picked up a book on geometry. He was just thirteen years old then.

Einstein got his first taste of serious mathematics from a Polish medical student who used to visit his home very often. The Pole became his informal tutor and triggered his interest in science and maths by giving him books on the subjects. Einstein's mind would absorb things very quickly and he would extrapolate the outcomes of experiments and observations of others. For instance, in one of the books given to him, the author imagined riding alongside a wire carrying electric current. Einstein went a step ahead and imagined what would it be like if one could run alongside a beam of light at the speed of light? Would it look stationary, as it was also a wave?

His deep thinking in the realm of relative motion prompted him to write his first scientific paper, 'Investigation of the State of Ether in Magnetic Fields', when he was just sixteen years old. This idea of relative motion was to be central to his thinking for the next several years.

Marriage and Personal Life

Einstein's stay in Zurich turned out to be some of his best days in life. It was here that he met his first wife, Mileva Maric. He also met many scientists and thinkers with whom he discussed the ideas and theories he was working on. He wanted to get married and support a family, but his father had gone bankrupt and he himself was jobless. His parents also did not approve of Mileva as she was a Serb and this added to his problems. In 1902, he got a job as a patent clerk in Bern, Switzerland. His father, before his death, gave Einstein the permission to marry the girl he loved and he got married in January 1903.

Einstein was four years younger than his wife. Mileva was his colleague, a mathematician and his companion in his work. She had a great influence on his theories and creative work. Their marriage was an intellectual partnership. As their family grew with two sons and a daughter (who died at a young age), Mileva had to leave the job she loved. Einstein knew that his wife was ambitious.

Though he admired her intellect and said that he was lucky to have someone who was his equal and as strong and independent as he was, in a span of a few years, there was trouble in their married life. In 1909, Einstein resigned from the patent office and joined the University of Zurich as a professor. Within a year they shifted to Prague, hoping for a better marital life, but soon returned to Zurich with bitterness lingering in their relationship.

At the beginning of World War II, Einstein accepted a job in Berlin and his relationship with Mileva further plunged to an all-time low. He started becoming very demanding, giving her a long list of rules to be followed at home. His affair with his first cousin only added to the woes and he decided to go for a separation. In 1919 Einstein and Mileva were divorced and he got married to his cousin Elsa.

Contribution to Science—and Humanity

In the patent office, Einstein honed the skill of grilling people about their ideas and inventions. He continued this job for seven years and became very good at articulating his questions and thoughts in simple words. It was to become one of his greatest assets for the rest of his life. Einstein had studied James Clerk Maxwell's theories of electromagnetic waves and had discovered that light travelled at a constant speed—a fact that was not even known to Maxwell himself. Coupled with Isaac Newton's idea of no absolute velocity, he started working on the theory of relativity.

The year 1905 was a year of miracles for Einstein. At the age of twenty-six, he was at his creative best. He submitted his thesis for a PhD, which was just twenty-four pages long! He also submitted four top-class scientific papers in rapid succession to be published in *Annalen der Physik*, one of the most respected scientific journals. All four of them—on the Brownian motion, photoelectric effect, special theory of relativity and the equivalence of mass and energy—changed the course of physics in the times to come. His famous equation $E=mc^2$ showed that a tiny mass of matter can be converted into an enormous quantity of energy. Max Planck, a famous and most respected scientist of that time, recognized Einstein's talent and soon all the doors to top teaching institutes opened for him. In 1921, he was given the Nobel Prize for explaining the photoelectric effect, as at that time the theory of relativity was still in its nascent stage. Soon after, he laid the foundation of cosmology and predicted that the universe is constantly expanding and is dynamic in nature.

Einstein's Theoretical Contributions

'Discovery consists of seeing what everybody has seen and thinking what nobody has thought.'
—Albert Szent-Gyorgyi

Albert Einstein could be called the most imaginative 'inventor scientist'. While most other scientists acted on certain observations, Einstein primarily imagined and created theories. For instance, Isaac Newton formulated the law of gravitation when he observed an apple falling from a tree. Similarly, Archimedes came up with the Archimedes Principle when he got into a bathtub and observed that a certain amount of water splashed out of the tub once he stepped into it.

While others thought along similar lines and their theories were mostly based on their observations, Einstein was different. He imagined. He imagined light, universe, time and motion before he formulated his theories about them. None of these concepts are easily perceivable by ordinary people or ordinary minds. In fact, he imagined the unimaginable.

Einstein was also a keen observer but he imagined certain things on the basis of 'What if…?' For example, he asked himself a question, 'What if I travel at the speed of light along a beam of light? Will the beam appear stationary?' This was the foundation of his theory of relativity.

His contribution to the field of modern physics is unparalleled. He established two pillars of modern physics—the theory of relativity and quantum mechanics.

Mass–energy equivalence: $E=mc^2$

$E=mc^2$ became the most popular equation that established a relation between mass and energy. This formula is also the foundation for atomic energy and atomic weapons. E is the energy released, m is the mass of the matter and c is the speed of light which is 300,000 kilometres per second, or 299,792,458 metres per second. The mass–energy equivalence was used to understand energy generated by nuclear fission chain reaction. Energy is calculated by the difference of mass of the nuclei that enter and exit a nuclear reaction. If we use kilogram to represent mass and speed of light in metres per second, then the energy released would be in joule (J).

For 1 kilogram matter, the energy equivalent will be E= $(299,792,458)^2 \times 1 = 9 \times 10^{16}$ J.

Therefore, for one gram, the energy equivalent will be around 90 terajoule (TJ), which is 21.5 billion kilocalories. This is equivalent to the energy released by combustion caused by 21.5 kilotons of TNT (trinitrotoluene).

In the atomic bomb that was dropped on Nagasaki, the fission caused by approximately 1 kilogram of the 6.15-kg plutonium resulted in becoming exactly 1 gram less after the fission process was complete. It therefore had the intensity of 21 kilotons of TNT explosion (thermal as well as blast energy).

This theory also throws light on the ability of the sun to produce heat and light continuously.

Special theory of relativity

Einstein's paper 'Electrodynamics of Moving Bodies' was later called the special theory of relativity. The motion of a body can only be described or perceived relative to something else or in reference to something else. These could be other bodies or a set of coordinates or an observer. These are called the 'frames of reference'.

The special theory of relativity extends this invariance or 'state of remaining unchanged' by introducing another dimension—time. Einstein also came up with relativity-based axioms like Doppler shift and addition law for velocities.

Nobel laureate Paul Dirac called general relativity 'probably the greatest scientific discovery ever made'; Max Born, another Nobel Prize-winning physicist, called it 'the greatest feat of human thinking about nature'.

Discovering the photoelectric effect

In 1900, Max Planck observed the radiation of light from hot bodies. When you take an iron rod and make it 'red-hot', it radiates light. This radiation can occur in discrete packets of energies called quanta (bundles) and not in any arbitrary amounts.

If Planck's hypothesis of quanta was applicable to radiation, Einstein concluded that it was also applicable to electrons being emitted by the metal on which light was impinged. This was known as the 'photoelectric effect'. Einstein received the Nobel Prize in 1921 for his 'law of the photoelectric effect' which laid the foundation for modern quantum theory.

As the genius theoretical physicist Stephen Hawking says, 'Time travel used to be thought of as just science fiction, but Einstein's general theory of relativity allows for the possibility that we could warp space-time so much that you could go off in a rocket and return before you set out.'

Bose-Einstein statistics and condensate—God particle

Bosons are one class of particles that draw their name from 'Bose'. In 1924–25, Satyendra Nath Bose, an Indian physicist, and Einstein, through quantum statistics, showed that at low temperatures bosons may reach discrete energy states and thus most of them could 'condense' into the same energy state.

Further research was done and in 2012 the Higgs boson, dubbed as the 'God particle', was discovered, leading it to super fluidity and zero viscosity.

Practical and Commercial Applications of Einstein's Discoveries

> *Any sufficiently advanced technology is indistinguishable from magic.*
> —Arthur C. Clarke

Albert Einstein investigated issues which, at that time, did not appear to directly impact any ordinary mortal. But all those who were in the field of fundamental physics could appreciate their impact in times to come. In fact, his ideas continue to have an impact even today, and will be relevant even in the future.

Today, our life revolves around electronics—something that is based entirely on fundamental physics. It is Einstein who laid the basis for 'applied electronics' and thus led to the making of many of the items we use every day.

Below are some of the inventions that came about because of fundamental physics, to which Einstein had contributed immensely.

Solid-state physics

This is a practical branch of physics, and probably the largest one, that studies the properties of matter at the atomic and subatomic levels. Many people don't know that the invention of electronic devices such as transistors, diodes, field-effect transistors, integrated circuits, transducers, capacitors and resistors is based on solid-state physics.

Transistor: The invention of transistors opened the floodgates for electronics and telecommunications. Solid-state devices thereafter ruled our lives and will continue to do so, maybe forever.

Laser: This is used for cutting any surface of an object precisely and also for laser printers. CD players use lasers to read data from the surface of a compact disc. In the field of medicine, laser surgery is used for very precise operations that makes surgery almost non-invasive.

Computers: In the 1950s, semiconductor devices gradually replaced the vacuum tubes, and that brought a quantum shift in the power and speed of computers. Computers became smaller, smarter and faster.

Telecom boom: Till the mid-1960s, telecommunication devices like exchanges and multiplexing systems used vacuum tubes. They were replaced by electronic exchanges and systems. Telecom was revolutionized by optical fibre, which enabled gigabits of bandwidth on a single fibre link. A computer was not just being used for calculations per se, but also for word processing, art work, animation, communication between different locations and much more. The basis of the entire telecom network, the

Internet and computing is quantum mechanics and fundamental physics.

Quantum computers: Researchers are hopeful that these computers can solve problems one can never imagine solving using the existing computers. Though the industry of quantum computers is in its infancy, the major thrust is to come up with machines that can crack problems which conventional computers would take centuries to solve. Besides Artificial Intelligence, it will help in medicine, forecasting, finance and cryptology.

Theory of relativity and Global Positioning System: Global Positioning System, or GPS, is a satellite-based navigation system where all the connected objects are in motion. The earth is rotating on its axis and also moving around the sun in an orbit. The satellites, a group of twenty-four, orbit around the earth at about 20,000 kms from earth's surface. They move at a speed of 14,000 kms per hour or more. The satellites carry an atomic clock, which has an accuracy of one billionth of a second. The GPS determines its position by comparing the signals it receives from these satellites and then arrives at a 'fix'. Here precision is important and an ordinary GPS mounted on a car gives you an accuracy of 5 to 10 metres.

For time accuracy, the theory of relativity plays an important role and clocks must be accurate to the time of twenty to thirty nanoseconds. Because the observer in the car on the ground sees the satellite in motion relative to him, the special theory of relativity says that it would see the satellite clock ticking more slowly. This would hamper obtaining the right position. The engineers who created GPS took special care to 'offset' this anomaly, thus making it a reliable and accurate system.

Atomic clocks: These are by far the most accurate timekeepers in the world and very stable. The long-term accuracy of atomic clocks is better than one second per one million years! Without these clocks there would be no way to maintain a centrally synchronized time; GPSes would not work and the position of planets for spacecraft applications would not be accurate enough. Quantum mechanics is again at the heart of this invention.

Nuclear energy: Nuclear or atomic energy is a huge source of energy which can be used for different, peaceful purposes.

Today, nuclear power electricity generated by nuclear power plants meets almost 15 per cent of the world's electricity demands, by generating more than 2500 TW.h or terawatt hour. One terawatt hour is equal to one billion kilowatt hours. Einstein's linkage of mass of matter to energy was the basis of nuclear chain reaction, releasing enormous heat energy that is now converted into electricity.

How these inventions affect our daily lives

When we go to malls for shopping, the stuff we buy gets billed through scanners. These as well as the digital cameras we use for clicking photos were invented based on Einstein's theories. His discovery of relativity had an impact on important inventions like the television. The sharp pictures we view are possible because of the theory of relativity. Mass of electrons that are accelerated in a TV increase substantially. If this was not taken into account, the images would be blurred.

Solar cells are based on his theory of photoelectric effect.

When Einstein was gaining popularity, Germany was witnessing a great change. The Nazis, under Adolf Hitler, were sweeping the political scene in Europe. By 1930, anti-Semitism and hatred for Jews was at its peak in Germany and Nazis started calling Einstein's theory of relativity as 'Jewish physics'. They started burning any literature created by Jews. Moreover, Jews were also banned from any government jobs and debarred from teaching in universities. Einstein was on their hitlist and, better sense prevailing, he decided not to settle down in Germany. By the end of 1932, he moved to America and left Germany for good. He was accepted with open arms at Princeton, which later became a Mecca of sorts for theoretical physics.

At the beginning of World War II, many scientists fled Germany and its allies and settled down in the US. They knew that the Nazis had started working on a new wonder weapon—an atom bomb. Some of them warned the US officials of this development but were not taken seriously. In the middle of 1939, just before the war started, Einstein wrote a letter to President Franklin Roosevelt, who invited him to discuss the situation and ordered research in this area. The initiative to develop an atom bomb was called Project Manhattan, which was triggered because of Einstein's letter to the President.

Albert Einstein was to taste the culture of meritocracy in the US, where a person was recognized for his abilities and was free to work as he or she felt like. He thrived on this and was able to give his best to the world in the field of theoretical physics.

Though Einstein was responsible for urging the American president to start research on the atom bomb, he was not at all involved in its research. But he contributed to the war effort in many different ways; one being his monetary contribution of

US$ 6.5 million by auctioning his manuscript of the theory of relativity. He was anguished to learn about the bombing of the twin cities, Nagasaki and Hiroshima, by the Americans. He began a protest to stop the production of atomic weapons.

Throughout his life he demonstrated a great sense of humour and wit. He came up with quotes on almost every subject that one can think of. His quotes are very famous and often used by many people even today.

Einstein spent his last days at Princeton. He died at the age of seventy-six on 18 April 1955 at the Princeton University medical centre. He was cremated, but his brain was removed and kept for study by neuroscientists in the future.

The next day after his death, as a tribute to this legend, the *Washington Post* carried a sketch of the cosmos in which the earth is identified by the label 'Albert Einstein lived here'.

'I have no special talent. I am only passionately curious.'
—Albert Einstein

1

BE ALTRUISTIC AND A SOCIAL ACTIVIST

Perform Philanthropic and Benevolent Acts

'It is every man's obligation to put back into the world at least the equivalent of what he takes out of it.'
—Albert Einstein

Giving Back to Society—an Attitude

Albert Einstein was not content with his contribution to science alone. He wanted to be a responsible citizen. Throughout his life, he spoke his mind on a variety of issues that were relevant to the well-being of his fellow citizens. He said, 'A hundred times every day I remind myself that my inner and outer life are based on the labours of other men, living and dead, and that I must exert myself in order to give in the same measure as I have received and am still receiving.' There was probably nobody in the scientific community who was so actively involved in public service and politics, at both the national as well as international level. He was a radical who participated in various movements and lent his support to causes that affected people. Be it the two World Wars; the Holocaust, where millions of Jews were killed; the bombing of Japan; the Cold War; apartheid; or the homeland for Jews—he actively participated in humanitarian movements during these events. Perhaps this was the main reason for his popularity and why he became a cult figure. It is intriguing and worth admiring that a man so deeply involved in the study of science could take out time for these activities—sometimes even risking his neck by sticking it out too far.

Einstein was a great admirer of Otto van Bismarck and advocated a social system that would provide security to all individuals and cater to their medical needs in case of illness. He was always against war, as he himself had witnessed two World Wars in his lifetime. He had gone through a great personal tragedy of being forced to leave his country and having to migrate to America to save his life and live in dignity. The roots of this humiliation were the wars between nations and divisive politics, and therefore he hated war and violence in any form.

A Proud Jew Who Helped his Community

When the anti-Semitism wave started gaining momentum, Einstein's Jewish background made him the target of the German political class. In Germany, his theory of relativity was rubbished as 'Jewish perversion' not only by politicians but also by fellow scientists. While his papers were burnt by the Nazis, the Germans also placed a huge cash award on his head. He had to take bodyguards for protection during his lecture tour in Europe. This triggered the idea of him settling down in the US, never to return to Germany. Einstein supported all organizations that stood up against the Nazis to protect Jews.

He was a proud Jew which is amply clear in his statement:

The pursuit of knowledge for its own sake, an almost fanatical love of justice and the desire for personal independence—these are the features of the Jewish tradition which make me thank my stars that I belong to it.

In Support of Equal Rights

Einstein was against any type of discrimination. Having acquired his American citizenship, he became very involved in the civil rights movement. He wanted people of all colours to get the same rights. He was against white supremacy, though he himself was a white German. While addressing students at the Princeton University in 1948 he said, 'There is, however, a sombre point in the social outlook of Americans. Their sense of equality and human dignity is mainly limited to men of white skins.' He was against fascism and kept asking the US government to allow Jewish refugees from Germany and other parts of occupied Europe to migrate to America. But the US government did not oblige him.

Opposed to Atomic Weapons and War

'I know not with what weapons World War III will be fought, but World War IV will be fought with sticks and stones.'
—Albert Einstein

The first atom bomb was dropped by the US on Japan on 6 August 1945, on the city of Hiroshima, and three days later on Nagasaki on 9 August 1945. This was the biggest devastation and human tragedy ever in the history of mankind, killing more than 200,000 people. Many people died instantly and many more died due to radiation sickness in the next several months.

Criticizing the war, Einstein said,

> He, who joyfully marches to music in rank and file, has already earned my contempt. He has been given a large brain by mistake, since for him the spinal cord would fully suffice. This disgrace to civilization should be done away with at once. Heroism at command, senseless brutality, deplorable love-of-country stance, how violently I hate all this, how despicable and ignoble war is; I would rather be torn to shreds than be a part of so base an action! It is my conviction that killing under the cloak of war is nothing but an act of murder.

Einstein and the Atom Bomb

Many people feel that Albert Einstein was the one who invented the atom bomb. This is far from true. Einstein was never involved in the research and development of the nuclear bomb by the US government. The project that was started by the US to develop a bomb was called 'Project Manhattan' and the government did not involve Einstein in this for several reasons. The major reason why Einstein was kept away from the project was because he was always against war and the then FBI director, J. Edgar Hoover, was against sharing this 'top secret' information with him. Hoover believed that Einstein could not be trusted with such a secret. In as early as 1929, when the German Nazi Party was planning to go to war with the rest of Europe, Einstein refused to join war service if a war broke out. Americans had studied his history well and were convinced not to involve him. Technically speaking though, Einstein had sown the seed and laid the foundation of nuclear energy. His equation $E=mc^2$

demonstrated that a vast amount of energy can be released by a small amount of matter if put through a chain reaction process, thus making a bomb theoretically a possibility.

Einstein did ask the US government to start research on the atom bomb

As Germany was preparing to go to war in 1938, German scientists were able to split the uranium atom and were on the threshold of starting research on the nuclear bomb.

The Hungarian-American physicists, Eugene P. Wigner and Leo Szilard, knew about this development in Germany and wanted to inform the highest officials in the US government to take up a research project for making a nuclear bomb. But they did not know how to go about it because they neither had any contacts in the government administration nor did they have adequate influence. At that time, Einstein was an international celebrity and had enough clout to influence the government and even reach the president of America—Franklin D. Roosevelt.

Einstein, at that time, was not even aware of the capability and consequences of a chain reaction. Leo Szilard and Einstein decided to inform the president and urged him to start nuclear research. The letter was drafted by Szilard, signed by Albert Einstein and sent to the US government. Later, it was sanctioned as Project Manhattan, and ultimately produced the atomic bombs that were dropped on Japan.

Einstein was not aware of nuclear particle physics that was required for the bomb, but he was knowledgeable in other associated areas; and, as explained earlier, for political reasons he was not a part of the research.

It was Vannevar Bush, a scientist working directly on Project

Manhattan, who approached Einstein for help. The American scientists were facing a problem related to the separation of isotopes that shared the same chemical and structural properties. Einstein used his skills in diffusion and osmosis to get the right solution, and cracked the problem in just two days. Therefore, his contribution towards the invention of the atomic bomb was minimal and in no way was he directly involved.

America would have invented the bomb even without Einstein's letter to the president, but then it would have not been ready during the World War II period.

The Nobel laureate's efforts to prevent nuclear proliferation

'The release of atomic power has changed everything except our way of thinking…the solution to this problem lies in the heart of mankind. If only I had known, I should have become a watchmaker.'

—Albert Einstein

Soon after the twin bombings in Japan in August 1945, the horror associated with atom bombs was evident. Einstein opposed nuclear proliferation and wanted governments to stop producing any more bombs. He also realized that the bombs had been produced to stop Nazi Germany from making them before the Americans did, and said on behalf of the physicists:

> Today the physicists who participate in watching the most formidable and dangerous weapon of all time…cannot desist from warning and warning again: we cannot and should not slacken in our efforts to make the nations of the world and especially their governments aware of the unspeakable disaster they are certain to provoke, unless they change their attitude towards each other and towards the task of shaping the future.

We helped in creating this new weapon in order to prevent the enemies of mankind from achieving it ahead of us. Which, given the mentality of the Nazis, would have meant inconceivable destruction, and the enslavement of the rest of the world.

On 19 August 1946, an article appeared on the front page of *New York Times* with the headline: 'Einstein Deplores Use of Atom Bomb'. The article further said: 'Professor Albert Einstein said that he was sure that President Roosevelt would have forbidden the atomic bombing of Hiroshima had he been alive.'

Five months before his death, Einstein told the world about his feelings and his participative role in inventing the atomic bomb when he wrote, 'I made one great mistake in my life, when I signed the letter to President Roosevelt recommending that atom bombs be made, but there was some justification—the danger that the Germans would make them if we don't.'

Einstein was against atomic bombs as he, along with many other scientists, knew the devastation it could cause. He was also aware that such a weapon would start an arms race between the US and the USSR. To lobby against this, they formed ECAS—Emergency Committee of Atomic Scientists—which was chaired by Einstein himself. They wanted atomic development under international control rather than being under any one country. Of course, this aim could never be achieved.

Einstein–Russell Manifesto, 1955

Bertrand Russell, a British philosopher, historian and social critic, along with Albert Einstein, spearheaded the effort to ban the development of nuclear weapons and usher in an environment of peace after the horrific experience of the six-year-long World War II. The scientist community feared that the public and world leaders were unaware of the implications of the newly developed hydrogen bombs.

On 9 July 1955, a few months before Einstein's death, Russell delivered a grave warning to avoid nuclear war in the future. It was signed by eleven eminent scientists including Einstein and was made public in front of the press.

Russell said:

> There lies before us, if we choose, continual progress in happiness, knowledge and wisdom. Shall we instead choose death, because we cannot forget our quarrels? I appeal as a human being to human beings; remember your humanity, and forget the rest. If you can do so, the way lies open to a new Paradise; if you cannot, there lies before you the risk of universal death.

Einstein Saved Many Jews from Being Killed by the Nazis

'Zionism springs from an even deeper motive than Jewish suffering. It is rooted in a Jewish spiritual tradition whose maintenance and development are for Jews the basis of their continued existence as a community.'

—Albert Einstein

Einstein was aware that the Nazis under Adolf Hitler would destroy the Jews. Therefore, he made extensive efforts to take as many Jews out of Germany as he could. He not only coordinated with other German Jews but also appreciated those who rallied behind his efforts.

Hyman Zinn was a New York-based businessman who

helped Jews escape Germany and Einstein wrote a letter of thanks to him. The letter, written in English, read:

> It must be a source of deep gratification to you to be making so important a contribution towards rescuing our fellow Jews from the calamitous peril and leading them towards better future. The power of resistance [that] has enabled the Jewish people to survive for thousands of years have [sic] been based to a large extent on traditions of mutual helpfulness. In these years of afflation [sic] our readiness to help one another is being put to a severe test. May we stand this test as well as did our fathers before us?

This letter to Zinn was recently auctioned. The reserve price for it was around US$5,000 to US$7,000, but eventually it sold at US$14,000!

Einstein Donated All that He Had

Albert Einstein made very good use of his celebrity status and used all the money he earned for philanthropy. He focused on rescuing German Jews, war survivors and also the education of youth. He readily lent his name for hospitals and colleges. He was a great teacher, kind and courteous to his fellow scientists and students. He was also against high tuition fees for the poor and often gave them free physics lessons. He also managed to switch roles easily—teaching at college in the morning and discussing politics and participating in related events in the evening.

As an individual, he empathized with the Jews and helped many of them escape Germany before Hitler and his Nazi Party came to power on 30 January 1933. He helped the Jewish community in whatever way he could. He started the Hebrew

University of Jerusalem and gave lectures in America to collect money for the university. The money received from his brand equity and sale of merchandise is used to provide higher education to thousands of students even today. He also bequeathed his writings and intellectual property to the Hebrew University. He was actively involved in raising funds for organizations like United Jewish Appeal and worked towards creating a Jewish homeland. Though he was always a staunch Jew, Einstein never wanted Jews to become too aggressive and kill others.

In 1933, on the suggestion of Einstein, the International Relief Association (IRA) was founded. It was created to assist Germans who suffered because of the Nazi Party, under Hitler. Later, in 1940, the assistance was extended to those who suffered under the fascist regime of Mussolini in Italy and Francisco Franco, the dictator of Spain. Several thousand political leaders, scientists and academicians were rescued by the IRA.

'People will forget what you said, people will forget what you did, but people will never forget how you made them feel.'
—Bonnie J. Wasmund

LESSONS FROM THE LIFE OF AN INNOVATIVE GENIUS

1. Make it a habit to give back to society. If you cannot provide monetary help, then give your services for free. If you are a teacher, spend some time to teach poor children.
2. Believe in equality. Give everyone an equal chance. Don't be biased by religion, caste or gender when it comes to judging people.
3. Help others as much as you can. Do charity; it gives a lot of satisfaction.

2

PRACTISE HUMILITY

Be Humble Even After Achieving Success

'If the quantum and the gates of time are the strongest features of this strange universe, and if they shall prove in time to come the doorways to that deeper view for which Einstein searched, mankind will forever remember with gratitude his absolutely decisive involvement with both.'
—John Archibald Wheeler

A Role Model for Generations to Come

Albert Einstein was born into a poor Jewish family. He was an average student in school, yet he attained the stature of one of the greatest scientists of the world. His achievements and spectacular success can motivate every ordinary or underachieving child to do well in life.

Einstein's theories were complex and had a deeper meaning which most ordinary people could not understand. Even the scientific community was in awe of his grip on science and depth of knowledge.

Therefore, the world looked up to him with respect. He raised the status of science in the eyes of ordinary people. Younger generations realized that education could change their lives; education was the ticket to success. Einstein became a cult figure, a household name, and with his influence he could sway national policy and opinions related to education, diversity, inclusiveness, human rights and even nuclear warfare.

At a philosophical level, Einstein changed the concept of 'absolute' to 'relative'. Nothing could be absolutely right or absolutely wrong. This has its grounds in day-to-day life as well; what was right ten years ago may not be right or relevant today. Scientific theories that were considered correct earlier have been proved wrong. For instance, the theory that the sun revolves around the earth or that the earth is flat. Therefore, even scientific theories are relative and not absolute.

Possibly one of the earliest examples of thinking 'relatively' is this famous anecdote of Akbar and his witty minister Birbal: Akbar asks Birbal to shorten the length of a line drawn on a paper without erasing it. Birbal quickly takes a pencil and alongside the line, draws another line that is longer than the existing one! He then says, 'Maharaj, now see, your line has become smaller.'

Despite having achieved name, fame and respect of the world which very few could achieve, Einstein was still very humble and down to earth.

Albert Einstein not only worked, researched and taught in his own style, but he also lived his life the way he wanted to. This may be true in the case of several creative people and thinkers who want to remain free from any 'societal shackles' as they really don't care what others think of them. Einstein loved music, and he especially liked playing his violin. He also tried his hand at the piano. He loved sailing, going out for long walks and spending time at home with his pets. He enjoyed the small gifts of life and never clamoured for big cars or a big home. He never showed off his status or stature. This is what we need to learn from great people—always keep your feet on the ground.

Unassuming and Down to Earth

Einstein embraced and befriended the great as well as the humble. He could strike a conversation with anyone regardless of that person's status or intellect. On one hand, he would be dealing with a complex problem in physics, and on the other, he would be playing the violin with a local grocer. He was at ease with kids as well.

One day, an eight-year-old neighbour in Princeton asked him if he could help her solve some mathematical problems and finish her homework. It was in the 1930s, by which time Einstein was one of the greatest scientists of the world. He could have easily shooed her out, but he told her, 'I would love to teach you, but then it would be unfair to the other girls in the school.' She was carrying a chocolate fudge for him, which he took and in return gave her a cookie. He would never show off that he was a celebrity.

He would accept invitations to speak at conferences and seminars without much fuss. Whenever he was invited to play the violin in an orchestra, he would readily agree, despite his celebrity status. This was one major reason for his being popular with the masses as well as the scientific community.

Einstein's ultimate sacrifice and display of being a simple man, looking for no rewards for his hard work and achievement, was demonstrated by his refusal to become the president of Israel. This was in recognition of his service to mankind in general and Jews in particular, by the Government of Israel.

Humbled by God's Creation

'The more I study science, the more I believe in God.'
—Albert Einstein

God is conceived and viewed as a supreme being, the Almighty and the highest object of faith. They say that when reason fails, faith begins. Since at times we cannot reason out what happens to us, our loved ones or our lives, and because we cannot look into the future or predict our destiny, we look up to that omnipresent being, the one who has infinite knowledge and unlimited power. The basic premise of our belief in the Almighty is our inability to predict our lives and control what is happening around us.

Many thinkers and philosophers have argued both against and for the existence of God. Different religions define God in their own ways, so that people are led on to a path of spirituality to connect with the Almighty. Different religions have given different names to God, making him more perceivable and acceptable to the common man. This gave rise to the idea of personal faith and a personal god. We are asked to pray to and acknowledge that power. Without seeing or understanding God, we pray. Prayer and faith have a placebo effect on our well-being.

Einstein looked at this Almighty or supreme power in a different way. In fact, he defined his own god and was nearer to God than most of us. He believed in the supreme power because he was humbled by the structure, the expanse and the unlimited energy he could perceive in the universe, in our very existence. He was humbled because he, having analysed matter, time, space and motion scientifically, realized how insignificantly small he was in front of God, who kept track of every event, every bit of matter and every life that existed in the vast universe, and was our keeper in the strictest sense.

While gurus and spiritual leaders understood and interpreted God through mythology and philosophy, Einstein interpreted God through science. He looked at God scientifically, in terms of our existence. He did not believe in any 'personal god', and as far as religion was concerned, he was religious because he was in the awe of God's creation the structure of the world, so far as science could reveal. He would look up to God for the harmony that exists in the universe.

Einstein realized, and made others realize, through his writings and talks, that as human beings we are just a part of this massive universe. It is only an illusion that we are separate entities; in actuality we are a part of one big whole, what we call the universe. His thoughts on and interpretation of the relation between God and an individual is philosophical and he describes it as an optical or visual delusion of consciousness. Almost a year before his death he had said that humans must break away from this delusion. This, according to him, becomes a prison of selfishness. He said, 'We must free ourselves from this bondage [of personal attachment] and widen our circle of compassion to embrace all living creatures and whole of nature and its beauty and obtain liberation from the self.'

Many saints and philosophers have preached what he said without really understanding the enormity of these words scientifically. But Einstein could also understand the power of nature scientifically. Even though he was an atheist, he felt and perceived the power of the Almighty. In fact, all saints and prophets are humbled by the Almighty in a philosophical way.

Whereas most preach fear of God, Einstein advocated being in awe of God.

Imagine, even an insignificant (size-wise) particle like an electron not only goes around the nucleus but also spins around its own axis! This is the tiniest example of nature's complexity and precision that has been created by God. On the other hand, look at our solar system, which is a part of the Milky Way galaxy, which has 200 to 400 billion stars. One estimate says that there are 100 to 200 billion such galaxies as ours in the universe, which means approximately 20,000 to 80,000 billion stars! Einstein possibly understood the hugeness of this entire universe, and our insignificance as individuals, and thus he believed in the superpower we call God. He was sure that the universe is an orderly place and God knows everything, every consequence.

Try stepping out into the open at night to look at the sky. You will realize that there are millions of stars in the sky, and when compared to the universe we, as individuals, are so insignificant and powerless. Leonardo da Vinci has rightly said, 'Human subtlety will never devise an invention more beautiful, more simple or more direct than does nature because in her inventions nothing is lacking, and nothing is superfluous.'

Having believed in the supreme power of nature, Einstein wrote a letter in 1954, a year before his death, where he called God and religion 'pretty childish'. He also ridiculed the idea that the Jews, the community he belonged to, were the 'chosen ones'. This handwritten letter in German, also dubbed as the 'God letter' by Einstein, was put up for auction on eBay; the first bidder offered US$3 million for it and it sold for a little over that amount.

Einstein also explained his concept of God in an analogy,

> I'm not an atheist, and I don't think I can call myself a pantheist. We are in the position of a little child entering a huge library filled with books in many languages. The child knows someone must have written those books. It does not know how. It does not understand the languages in which they are written. The child dimly suspects a mysterious order in the arrangement of the books but doesn't know what it is. That, it seems to me, is the attitude of even the most intelligent human being toward God. We see the universe marvellously arranged and obeying certain laws but only dimly understand these laws. Our limited minds grasp the mysterious force that moves the constellations.

One can appreciate the simplicity of these words and yet their striking ability in getting the point across. Einstein could articulate and explain the most complex things in the simplest way possible.

One thing that Einstein learnt through his understanding of the universe was that it was beyond human comprehension, it appeared ever-expanding and limitless. In most of his discussions, this aspect was reflected in one form or the other. He once said that what he saw in nature was a magnificent structure, which we comprehend very imperfectly. Any thinking person would be engulfed with a feeling of humility and insignificance before it. This was, according to him, a religious feeling based on logic and not mysticism. He had genuine respect for the might of nature. I quote him below:

> A knowledge of the existence of something we cannot penetrate, of the manifestations of the profoundest reason and the most radiant beauty, which are only accessible to our reason in their

most elementary forms—it is this knowledge and this emotion that constitute the truly religious attitude; in this sense, and in this alone, I am a deeply religious man.

Once, a child wrote to him, asking if scientists ever prayed. He wrote back, 'God does not care about our mathematical difficulties. He integrates empirically.' He explained his standpoint further by saying that according to science, everything that takes place is as per the laws of nature. Therefore a scientist could not believe that events could be influenced by a wish addressed to a supernatural being in the form of a prayer. But our knowledge of these laws is also imperfect and based on our faith, in a way. Therefore, most serious scientists become convinced that a spirit is manifest in the laws of nature—a spirit vastly superior to that of man, in the face of which we, with our modest powers, must feel humble. This, he said, was a religious feeling of a special sort, different from the religiosity of someone more naïve! As they say, 'Where reason fails, faith begins.' In one sentence Einstein summed up the enormity of the universe when he said, 'There is no hitching post in the universe—so far as we know.'

Einstein believed that the universe could not be tied and kept limited—it was limitless.

'I believe that a simple and unassuming manner of life is best for everyone, best both for the body and the mind.'
—Albert Einstein

LESSONS FROM THE LIFE OF AN INNOVATIVE GENIUS

1. Keep your head in the clouds but your feet firmly on the ground.
2. If you are humble, people will respect you.
3. It is important to realize that as individuals we are tiny drops in the ocean as far as our existence in this universe is concerned. Therefore, do your best and never be arrogant.

3

SIMPLE LIVING, HIGH THINKING

Simplify Your Life and Don't Chase Money

'A table, a chair, a bowl of fruit and a violin; what else does a man need to be happy?'
—Albert Einstein

Jean Jacques Rousseau's famous quote: 'Man is born free, and everywhere he is in chains', can be interpreted in different ways. One interpretation is that modern states repress the physical freedom that is a man's birthright. Civil society, which came into existence for the preservation and benefit of the state as well as the citizens, eventually got a vice-like grip on individuals, who felt that their freedom was being snatched from them.

The other interpretation is that man has tied himself in chains because of his own deeds and needs. Modern lifestyle has provided us with the things we may not even need and yet, since these attractive things are available, we make efforts to acquire them, whatever be the price. This starts a vicious circle. To acquire these worldly pleasures we want more and more money, which translates into hard work, borrowing and getting tied up in monthly EMIs for many years.

People who become successful start looking for larger houses, fatter salaries, bigger cars and more expensive clothes. This is a rat race, and as they say: even if you win a rat race, you are still a rat. Today, big brands use celebrities and actors as their brand ambassadors to endorse their products and entice customers. Customers are enamoured by these role models and want to emulate them by using what they do.

Are there any role models who exude simplicity, and who have their feet firmly planted on the ground? Yes there are, but very few. Albert Einstein is one such, who demonstrated that despite being the greatest scientist of his time, he could lead a simple life. He had no airs about himself and very few personal needs. He enjoyed the little things in life and had no greed whatsoever.

> *'In order to form an immaculate member of a flock of sheep one must, above all, be a sheep.'*
> —Albert Einstein

Einstein never bothered about his looks, nor did he buy clothes that were classy or expensive. Most of the times he wore a grey suit. In fact, he bought several versions of the same grey suit because he didn't want to waste his time choosing what to wear each morning. Mark Zuckerberg, the founder and CEO of Facebook, though a billionaire, also wears almost identical T-shirts every day. Even Steve Jobs, the late co-founder of Apple, wore black turtleneck T-shirts and blue jeans as his signature style. Famous Indian lyricist Gulzar is always dressed in a starched white kurta-pajama. The most important lesson one can learn from these people is that being brand conscious is a sign of an inferiority complex. Great people don't bother about looking great, they actually believe in being great. Leonardo da Vinci rightly said, 'Simplicity is the ultimate sophistication.' Billionaires like Warren Buffet still don't use a cellphone, live in an ordinary house and love their simple meals and a game of cards with friends.

If you are good at your job, confident and composed, you need not invest in expensive, flashy clothes to impress people. It reminds me of the famous dialogue by Amitabh Bachchan, '*Hum jahan khade ho jaate hain, line wahin se shuru hoti hai.*'

Albert Einstein didn't purposely become casual about his dressing after becoming famous. He was like that from the very beginning—paying more attention to his work than clothes.

He never wore socks for two reasons. Firstly, he said that if you wear shoes, there is no need of socks and vice-versa because one of them is good enough. Secondly, he felt that after regular use, socks would have holes in them, which was very annoying. He didn't wear socks even when he went to meet the American president at the White House! It is said that when his wife would ask him to dress up properly while going to work, he would retort, 'Why should I, there everybody knows who I am!' Whereas while going for a big conference, when his wife asked him to wear something special, he said, 'No one knows me there, so it doesn't matter.'

When we go out for a party or dinner, we take so much care deciding what kind of shoes and matching socks we should wear, but if you analyse carefully, in a big crowd, nobody has the time to notice what you are wearing.

He Didn't Bother about Money

Being a world-famous celebrity and Nobel laureate did not go to his head. Towards his students and the young people who wanted to ask his opinion, he was very unassuming and approachable. He didn't care much about money. Once when he was given a cheque of US$1,500 by the Rockefeller Foundation, he used it as a bookmark and carelessly lost the book. He gave his Nobel Prize money to charity. He believed in charity and said, 'The value of a man resides in what he gives and not in what he is capable of receiving.' Yet, he was clear that one should not give away everything so that people don't use you like a punching bag.

Many feel that intelligent people are a little weird when it comes to their attitude and behaviour. In case of Albert Einstein, this was very true. He had several habits which were his trademark. For instance, his glass-noodle-like dishevelled hair, which he rarely combed, was his unique feature, and went very well with his professor's image. His hairstyle had no match. He had several other traits too which he demonstrated unabashedly. He attributed his carefree attitude and simple living to the fact that he had better and more important things to do than waste time in combing his hair, choosing clothes or even polishing his shoes. He was a 'no-nonsense' kind of a person, who always fired from the hip and never really cared about being politically correct. He had no pretensions and no hypocrisies.

He Never Wanted a Big Salary

When Einstein joined the faculty at Princeton University, he was asked to suggest his own remuneration. Abraham Flexner, the founder of Institute for Advanced Studies at Princeton, was expecting Einstein to demand a huge compensation, as by then, i.e. in 1937, he was a world-famous scientist and a Nobel Prize winner. But he was surprised, and to some extent dismayed, by what Einstein said he would require to live well. No American scholar would have settled for what he had asked as his pay. Einstein suggested a salary of US$3,000 per annum, which, if calculated at today's rate would be around US$48,000. Abraham Flexner did not accept this and made an offer of US$10,000, which was the minimum salary at which he would have hired any American scholar. Einstein's pension was fixed at US$7,500, which he refused as he found it too generous and had it reduced to US$6,000 per annum. This is a trait very rarely found in people.

His Worldly Possessions Were Limited

Einstein never owned a car, and never learnt how to drive. He lived in a two-storeyed house, which was the only property he had. This house was near the institute and he walked to work every day; he had few worldly possessions. He was not even in favour of high rates of interest and famously said, 'Compound interest is the eighth wonder of the world. He who understands it earns it…he who doesn't…pays it.'

He loved music and loved his violin. Once he was offered an expensive Guarneri violin as a gift, which he politely refused saying, 'Such great instruments must be used only by experts who could use its power and complexity.' Such was the genuineness of his simplicity.

'Life is really simple, but we insist on making it complicated.'
—Confucius

LESSONS FROM THE LIFE OF AN INNOVATIVE GENIUS

1. In today's fast-paced world, electronic gadgets can make our lives complicated and stressful. Learn to simplify your life by keeping away from these gadgets for some time every day.
2. Money is important for comfortable living, but don't run after it and make your life miserable.
3. Never link your status and self-esteem with money and worldly possessions. This will give you peace of mind and a healthy life.

4

COLLABORATE

Getting Along with People and Social Networking

'Alone we can do so little; together we can do so much.'
—Helen Keller

How Important Is Social Networking?

Today no company, no business, no individual can work in isolation and succeed. MNCs and corporate giants collaborate with others to leverage their strength. Business models are created to integrate with other existing models to enhance market presence, push up sales and also co-brand products for better visibility. Consultants and professionals need to work, and work with others, to get business.

On the other hand, scientists, music composers, philosophers, artists and writers are seen as individual islands of excellence who work in ivory towers. The question is, do they require 'other-worldly skills' to move forward in life, personally as well as professionally? Do they need to interact with others?

Scientists can very well work as individuals and may not

necessarily need to work with others. In Einstein's case, too, he worked in isolation in his initial days, which were probably the most productive years of his life—1905 being the year of reckoning for him.

After living with the idea of intelligence quotient (IQ) for almost eighty years, the world was given a new concept of multiple intelligences by Howard Gardner in 1983. Yet again, in 1995, Daniel Goleman put forth the idea of emotional intelligence (EI), which was accepted in no time. It takes into account the ability of a person to perceive and interpret his own emotions. How well he can manage his moods and emotions becomes another parameter of emotional excellence.

In addition, emotional intelligence assesses a person's ability to understand other people's emotional states and deal with them effectively, which is also popularly known as social intelligence. Though scientists like Einstein work in isolation, they need to exist as a part of society and therefore have no choice but to deal with people on day-to-day basis. Even at his workplace, for instance, Einstein had to often consult others and collaborate with some to augment his research work. While teaching at Princeton or lecturing across the world, he had to deal with students or distinguished audience members. It was important for him to have qualities like self-control, moral courage, empathy for others, delayed gratification and even the art of making friends.

One cannot attribute Einstein's spectacular success only to his high IQ. He had some other wonderful traits that would fall under the EI umbrella. These traits were equally important for his success and his fame as one of the greatest scientists of all time. How did he become so famous whereas other scientists of his time didn't? To a large extent his 'other qualities' were responsible for his phenomenal success. One of these qualities was his ability to befriend great minds and collaborate with fellow scientists in his research work.

Einstein had a number of 'close friends' because he was comfortable with anyone with an intellectual level matching his own. He never particularly sought the company of influential academicians or scientists, but the law of attraction worked for him as there is general affinity between like-minded people. Even his first wife was a scientist, and their association was professional first and personal later.

He often discussed his ideas with his friends and colleagues at the patent office at Bern. He had three friends at work—Michele Basso, Joseph Sauter and Lucien Chavan—and together they formed a physics group.

By pure chance he also struck up a close, life-long relationship with a Romanian student. Once he landed up at Bern, he decided to take tuitions and earn some money and accordingly placed an advertisement for physics and mathematics classes in the local newspaper. Maurice Solovine responded to this advertisement and very soon they developed a good friendship. Einstein realized that he enjoyed discussing philosophy with Maurice more than teaching him mathematics and physics. Gradually their discussions became pithy; they read books together and discussed great philosophers and their ideas. They also had another friend, Conrad Habicht, as a part of this philosophy group. Habicht was a mathematician and Einstein made use of his knowledge to soundboard the four famous papers that he prepared in 1905.

This philosophy group was named 'The Olympian Academy'

and Einstein was its president. Later, Maurice became a well-known philosopher and mathematician and remained a close friend of Einstein till his last days.

Einstein also collaborated with a number of scientists of his time and consulted them on various issues. Nathan Rosen, Peter Bergmann and Leopold Infeld were some of his long-term associates. In 1935, Einstein collaborated with Boris Podolsky, an American physicist of Russian-Jewish descent on 'mechanical description of physical reality'. He also co-opted Nathan Rosen and consulted Neil Bohr for several years before publishing their findings. This quality of Einstein may have been one of the reasons for his tremendous popularity. He could get along with others easily and that is why people liked him and talked about him much more than any other scientist of his time.

As Michele Jennae has said, 'Networking is not about just connecting people. It's about connecting people with people, people with ideas, and people with opportunities.'

Fusion of Minds

Many great minds left Germany when Hitler came to power. Thereafter, the mecca of science too shifted from Germany to the United States. The Institute of Advanced Studies at Princeton, founded in 1930, became the most intensive research centre in the world. Albert Einstein was almost like the 'Pope of Physics'. He lived just a mile and a half away and walked to the institute every day. He told his friends that this was the place where he found peace and experienced the feeling of 'hibernating like a bear in his cave'.

This was a place for intellectual minds to meet. Most scientists, researchers and physicists were connected to this centre and it provided a healthy platform for exchanging ideas, views and theories amongst the intellectuals. No wonder, great strides in pure science happened at Princeton's Institute of Advanced Studies.

Governments of leading nations constitute 'think tanks' within educational institutes of repute with the aim of getting independent third-party views on matters of public policy, economics, science and technology. Very useful potent ideas flow out of this process. It is possible to get quality output because the academic fraternity is free from day-to-day administrative and political pressures, which gives them uninterrupted free time to ponder over knotty problems.

It is important, at an individual level, to keep the right company and team up with people who are equal or even better than you. In schools and colleges, students who team up with good, hard-working and inspiring classmates do better in life. Enthusiasm and even intellect is infectious. I always tell my students, 'If you want to improve your game of tennis, play with a better player.'

Einstein's Important Collaborative Projects

A person of Einstein's stature and calibre would have found it difficult to work with other scientists of his time. But he worked in collaboration with many of his colleagues and even his students, as long as his work was exciting and the results were fruitful. He worked with Satyendra Nath Bose, Nathan Rosen, and even his former student Leo Szilard on a refrigerator. He was open to discussion at forums and forthright in discussing his problems and solutions with other scientists of his time.

One of the biggest lessons one can learn from Einstein is the beauty of diversity and ability to get involved in different areas of research.

Great actors don't stick to stereotyped roles. They experiment with positive as well as negative roles. Good actors look for challenges in their careers. They like to portray different characters, sometimes even risking their acting career by accepting offbeat roles. Similarly, good authors write on a variety of topics. In case of music directors, singers and even stand-up comedians, variety is the spice of life. All those who turn out to be great experiment with different genres. For Einstein, too, variety was the driving force.

'If I have seen further, it is by standing on the shoulders of giants.'
—Isaac Newton

LESSONS FROM THE LIFE OF AN INNOVATIVE GENIUS

1. Regardless of your profession, teamwork is important for success.
2. Nurture the habit of making friends, in school, college as well as your workplace.
3. Work with people who are good, honest and competent. You can learn a lot from them.

5

AWAKEN YOUR IMAGINATION

The Mind's Eye

'Science does not know its debt to imagination.'
—Ralph Waldo Emerson

What Is Imagination?

According to the dictionary, imagination is the ability to form new images, which are not perceivable by human senses. Therefore, what we hear, see, touch or feel is not imagination. Imagination also denotes creating something that does not exist. It could also mean to concoct something that is fabricated or fictitious. Note that the word fiction comes out of fictitious. Do animals concoct stories to deceive us? They do not have the capability to do this, so they don't. In comparison we, as humans, are very good at fabricating stories and can use it to our advantage. The most powerful thing about imagination is that it has no limits, no boundaries. That is why a human being could imagine being on the moon, or being able to fly. He could also imagine what could be at the centre of the earth. That is how Jules Verne wrote *Journey to the Centre of the Earth* (1864) without ever being there.

Imagination and creativity can be used in any field of human development. For instance, nowadays computer software has become so powerful that computers can make real almost anything conceived by our imagination. For example, an application like Facebook came into existence because someone said: 'Imagine how people will feel when they have an option to choose from "Hot or Not" when they will see two photos placed next to each other?' This figment of imagination gave birth to the social networking industry.

As a saying goes, a watermelon is a lemon that took a chance!

Imagination Is Our Greatest Strength

Human beings and chimpanzee have 98 per cent identical DNA. Yet chimps are chimps and humans are humans—very different from one another. One major reason for this huge difference is that chimps cannot imagine but humans can. Chimps can smell, feel pain, become emotional and attached to fellow beings and even recognize people and things. But they cannot create a story or a fictitious plot. This quality is our greatest strength. We can also choose better because we can imagine. When we are faced with a choice, we quickly imagine the consequences of our choices. We thus have the ability to make decisions that lead to better consequences.

Imagination Outweighs IQ, EI and Knowledge

IQ is related to logical thinking and the linguistic part of our abilities. EI looks at abilities like interpersonal skills, understanding each other's emotions and understanding our own emotions. Having knowledge means knowing facts and figures, having information, possessing data and also having practical as well as theoretical know-how.

None of the above is related to imagination or our ability to think up what has not been thought—the ability to create what does not exist.

As Einstein said, 'Imagination is more important than knowledge.'

A computer can be taught logic. It can be programmed to handle languages, text, translations, synonyms and also to perform spell check. It can measure distances, like in a GPS. It can be taught to move around using robotics and perform even precision surgery. It can synthesize music according to pre-programmed instructions.

You can even programme programs to programme programs! These are computer programs which can write programs for you, according to what you want. But you can never teach or programme a computer to imagine.

If we could teach computers to imagine or fantasize or be creative, we could have created or cloned a Wolfgang Mozart, a Stephen Hawking, a Confucius, an Einstein, an Arthur Hailey, a Robin Cook, an Ayn Rand, a Jules Verne or even an H.G. Wells.

> *'Scientists may have sophisticated laboratories,*
> *But never forget "eureka" was inspired in a bathtub.'*
> —Toba Beta

Imagination Is the Seed for Innovation, Invention and Creativity

Imagination is the key to creativity and innovation. When an artist picks up a palette with dozens of colours, it is difficult to imagine what he will eventually create. You cannot penetrate his imagination till he draws something on the canvas. Therefore, the more you can imagine, the more creative you become.

Knowledge and imagination are loosely related. You cannot imagine in a 'total vacuum'. You need to have a frame of reference. For instance, if you do not know what is light, you cannot imagine what it is made of or what it contains or how fast it travels.

Another way of looking at the connection between imagination and knowledge is reviewing a simple act that we often witness on TV shows or even during a live show like a quiz competition. In a quiz competition, sometimes the audience is shown a blurred picture of a celebrity on the screen and asked to identify the person. When someone from the audience identifies the person in the picture as 'Amitabh Bachchan', how does he know that it is his picture and not someone else's?

First, the person knows that there is someone called Amitabh Bachchan and how he looks. Second, he uses his imagination to 'fill in the blanks' to arrive at the complete picture. He imagines that the picture is of Amitabh Bachchan and nobody else.

Similarly, our mind can organize stimuli or outside triggers into a new pattern and form a 'future memory'. This can come up with ideas, events and predictions that have never existed before. Therefore, old experiences and knowledge stored in our brain can create a fusion and throw up new ideas or hypotheses.

I firmly believe that unless you think, you cannot think.

How to Become More Imaginative, like Einstein

Can someone be taught how to imagine or how to improve his imaginative ability? It is a complex question which is as tricky as asking someone, 'Are leaders born or made?' Leaders are born as well as made or trained. Working with great leaders can be infectious. You can imitate and also acquire some of their traits by staying and working with them. Teaching leadership in a classroom might be difficult, but leadership can be learnt by practice.

Art, too, can be taught to those who have a knack for it. If someone cannot even draw, how can he be taught how to paint? Artistic streak is something one is born with. If you do not have that in you and try to learn from a teacher, you may not become a great artist, but you will be able to learn the basics of drawing. Gradually, with effort and practice, you can keep improving. Therefore, whether it is leadership or art, both can be learnt to some extent.

How do people get ideas? This is a question which is impossible to answer. It is not possible to create ideas deliberately. Getting new ideas is the key to success in today's world and yet there are no simple methods to do so. God has been kind to all of us and each one of us has been gifted with the ability to imagine. For instance, we are afraid of darkness because we imagine something dangerous out there, lurking in the dark. We imagine a ghost, a witch or some person who can hurt us. Therefore, we all have the ability to imagine. Imagination is like a muscle, the more you use it, the more it develops. The more you try to imagine, the more imaginative you will become.

Serendipity means discovering something by accident. Some say it comes out of a subconscious mind. Many ideas come to us for no rhyme or reason. If some of the ideas you get are good, then you must learn to preserve them.

To stretch your imagination is to stretch your mind or do some kind of mental gymnastics. One simple technique I use very effectively in my class is to expand or contract a story.

Take the example of 'The Emperor's New Clothes', a story most of us have read. Two weavers promise an emperor an invisible suit, and when he goes out in public wearing the suit, a child says, 'He is not wearing any clothes at all!'

If a student is asked to narrate this story, it may take him just one minute to do so. But what if he is asked to expand it to five minutes by adding his own inputs, without diluting or deviating from the story, and yet keep it interesting? In such a situation, the student will fill in extra details to stretch the story.

For instance he might say, 'A king lived in a huge palace in Barcelona and had a large kingdom with one million subjects under him. He had a beautiful queen and two handsome sons. He had ten ministers, whom he set the task of getting him an invisible suit. One of the ministers named Alejandro sent his men, who hunted for ten days to locate ten tailors for the job.'

These details can go on and on. And thus, the same story can become ten minutes long. Adding details requires imagination. As a second exercise, I ask the students to compress a two-minute story into thirty seconds. This also requires imagination. This exercise not only teaches you to think, create and imagine, but also teaches you how to articulate.

Reading literature, especially fiction of all genres, helps to improve one's ability to imagine. I make sure that every student of my institute gets into the habit of reading fiction. Every student has to buy one book every month to build his/her personal library. Each student reads fantasy, crime, horror, mystery, biography, romance and even science fiction. This not only broadens their knowledge, it also improves their expressions and adds to their imaginative skills.

For instance, when you read a murder mystery, there is a plot you are urged to imagine. Something like: 'What is in the box in the underground cellar?' Or 'What is kept behind that curtain in the attic?'

> *'Imagination is not only the uniquely human capacity to envision that which is not, and, therefore, the foundation of all invention and innovation. In its arguably most transformative and revelatory capacity, it is the power that enables us to empathize with humans whose experiences we have never shared.'*
> —J.K. Rowling

Simple Ways to Fire Your Imagination

Expand your activity horizon—kick your comfort zone

Imagination gets locked up if your mind remains 'one-track'. Therefore, move out of your comfort zone. Engineering professionals, for instance, must spend some time on other disciplines as well. They must read poetry, try their hand at painting and read books of different genres. In a nutshell, become as diverse as possible in your interests.

Observe-think-observe

Most information goes into our minds through the visual mode. The more you observe, the more fertile your mind will be. You could be simply sitting at your window, looking at the street down below, where people are walking around or involved in different activities. Watch what they are doing; wonder why they are doing what they are doing. While observing all this, you may get a great idea that is worth working on. When you observe without straining your mind, a new idea may get triggered in your mind, something which could be absolutely fresh.

In an interview, music directors Dilip Sen and Sameer Sen recalled an incident regarding their famous Bollywood song '*Jab bhi koi ladki dekhun mera dil diwana bole, Ole Ole...*' from the film *Yeh Dillagi* (1994). They had been struggling for a punch line for a song and in utter disappointment, parked their car near a beach in Mumbai to take a break. Suddenly a hailstorm began and one of them, reacting to the falling hailstones, yelled, '*Oye dekh, ole*' and they started humming '*Ole, Ole, Ole*'. That is how this tune was created.

This story shows us that mere observation can trigger unexpected ideas.

Hobbies trigger imagination

Any new activity helps in making us more imaginative. Pick up anything that interests you; it could be photography, cooking, writing, dancing, digital art, magic, sculpting or even stand-up comedy.

Quiet time and daydreaming

This tops the list. Cognitive psychologist Jerome Singer calls daydreaming our default mental state. He goes on to say that we have two mental networks—one is daydreaming and the other is working memory. The two cannot operate at the same time. When our daydreaming network is on, the working memory is shut off and vice versa. Daydreaming—when your mind is totally free—is the most productive time for generating new ideas. According to a research conducted by Scott Barry Kaufman, a psychologist, and Mary Helen Immordino-Yang, a neuroscientist, while daydreaming (vacant mind), extremely productive neurological process is taking place. John Lubbock, a nineteenth-century thinker, said, 'Rest is no idleness, and to lie sometimes on the grass, under a tree, listening to trickling water, watching the clouds is not a waste of time.' This is also called 'constructive internal reflection'.

> 'When I am, as it were, completely myself, entirely alone, and of good cheer—say, travelling in a carriage, or walking after a good meal, or during the night when I cannot sleep; it is on such occasions that my ideas flow best and most abundantly.'
>
> —Mozart

Einstein Made the Best of Daydreaming

Though Einstein had a regular work schedule, he took time out for long walks on the beach or in the college campus. He said that while he was walking, he had that peace of mind and uninterrupted time when he could listen to and concentrate on what was going on in his head. For him, this was like a meditation session where he was all by himself, concentrating inwardly and listening to his own mind. When he could not go for a walk and was stuck with a puzzle, he would simply lie down on his bed and look at the ceiling, imagining and thinking about his work.

He found solace as well as stimulation in solitude. Saints use solitude to connect with themselves, and experience spiritual awakening, bringing them closer to God. Gautama Buddha attained enlightenment through meditation in an isolated spot.

Pablo Picasso, one of the greatest artists of all time, said, 'Without great solitude, no serious work is possible.'

Consume less and create more

Today, we are overloaded with information. Our minds are occupied all the time with TVs, computers or cellphones. If our mind is busy consuming all the time, when will it be free to create or imagine? Therefore, try and detoxify your mind by spending some time every day without using these electronic devices. Remember, too much information numbs the mind.

Visualize images

Soccer genius Wayne Rooney practises the next-day match in his mind. He finds out his own team's colours and those of the opponents and then paints a game situation in his mind, working out different combinations and strategies. During the actual match, when he is in that condition, the pre-planned solution comes to his mind.

Peep into the future

Dr Eric Heseltine, a neuroscientist, has said that visualizing how today's best machines could be used in the future as ordinary machines gives a tremendous leverage to futuristic thinking. As yesterday's mainframes are today's laptops, tomorrow's laptops will be as powerful as today's super computers and the next-generation cellphones. Today's iPhones have more computing power than a super computer of the 1980s. One day, a super computer may become a 'thumb top'. Therefore, if you develop futuristic software and test it on a super computer today, it will be able to run on a laptop a few years hence. This is extrapolative imagination.

Break away from functionality crisis

Don't think that a hammer can only be used to hit a nail or a screwdriver can only drive in a screw. Imagine ten ways in which you could use the hammer. The concept of 'jugaad' uses the same technique. With jugaad, you can fry an egg on a clothes' iron or even use a lighter to open a beer bottle.

Meditate

Meditation liberates our subconscious mind, the seat of imagination.

The Audacity of Imagination: Creative Minds

Creative people are those who have the ability to imagine more than ordinary people.

Authors and writers depend on imagination

Creative writers are very imaginative people. Those who write fiction need to come up with a 'story' or a plot which is original and new. They have to imagine characters, people, situations, locations and even an era. *Jurassic Park* (1993) was the creation of a mind that takes you to the prehistoric era. There are authors who write 'period stories'—stories set in a bygone era. Here again, the author works on a backdrop which he has learnt from history (knowledge), but he concocts a story by creating images and imaginary people who play through that story.

Then there are authors who create fast-paced fantasies which take us into another world. Look at the success of the Harry Potter series; it was a novel with imaginary characters. This is a world of fantasy, where the author and the reader both have to imagine. Most of the times, books are much more impactful than their movie adaptions. The reason is that in a movie, it is the director's vision that you see—which is limited to his own imagination. Whereas in a book, a reader can imagine the way he wants to. For example, a dark alley written about in a book can be imagined in a thousand different ways by a reader, but when shown in the movie, it is interpreted by the film director in a particular way.

Mythologies are liked by people because they are based on popular beliefs. Sometimes these are distortions of real historical events. Oftentimes, mythologies are mixed with religion, faith or culture. A lot is imagined by the creator of mythologies and a lot more is imagined by the reader to transport him into another world.

Another kind of people who have vivid imagination are those who peep into the future. They are mostly writers of sci-fi, or science fiction. Here, the author goes forward in time, say a hundred years from the present, and portrays people, their lives and challenges, all based in the future. Therefore, storytelling is one of the most potent ways of looking at imagination.

Musicians are imaginative

Music knows no boundaries, it follows no language or religion and that is why it is universal. Music requires imagination of a different type from what is required in other fields of art or science.

Aaron Copland, in his book *Music and Imagination* (1952), gives an excellent explanation of how imagination is important for a composer who creates music. He says, 'At no point can you seize the musical experience and hold it. You can do it in a film by stopping it and looking at a still shot which immobilizes a whole scene, it captures the whole scene. But in music if you stop it, it may capture just one chord or one note, which is meaningless!' He goes on to say, 'This never-ending flow of music forces us to use our imagination, because music is in a continual state of becoming or being created.' Poetry, some say, is reflective and makes one stop to think; but music is immediate, it becomes.

Copland also says, 'The more I live the life of music the more I am convinced that it is the freely imaginative mind that is at the core of all vital music-making and even listening.' He also reflects upon a very important aspect of creating music: 'Imaginative mind is essential for creating music, because music provides the broadest vista for imagination since it is the freest, the most abstract, the least filtered of all the arts, allowing uninterrupted and intuitive functioning of the imaginative mind.'

No wonder Einstein was also fond of music; he felt that playing the violin and the piano boosted his mental faculties.

A.R. Rahman, known as the Mozart of Madras, has won an Oscar for his musical contribution. For him, music liberates the listener and leads him into a frame of mind where he feels elevated. At Chennai, he has started a teaching initiative for those who want to learn and create world class music. He wants to give his students the necessary skills so that they can create their own palette of sounds rather following any set formula. He says, 'I want my students to be as imaginative as they like and my aim is to expand sensibilities.'

Music expands sensibilities

In his book *Frames of Mind* (1983), Howard Gardner dwells on the multiple intelligence theory, where he argues that human capacity cannot be measured in terms of one intelligence alone. A human being has several competencies which are 'standalone' in their own right and each one represents a specific 'intelligence domain'; music is one of them. He goes on to say that musical intelligence, being inherent, emerges very early in an individual. The music bug bit Einstein when he was just six years old. In his case, it developed further because of the initiative taken by his mother.

In his research, Gardner also discovers that musical intelligence can constructively interact with other human intellectual competencies. Since musicians constantly hum in their minds, they have tones in their heads, which keeps their mind alert to picking up 'other things' from the environment. Most musicians play by the ear, and also have to be patient listeners if they have to grasp something out of existing music. This helps them develop the ability to become good, observant listeners.

To further determine the link between music and other competences, Howard Gardner says that musical faculty can be enhanced simply by the exploration of the oral and aural channels. Anthropologist Levi Strauss says, 'If we can explain music and intelligence related to it, we may be able to find the key for all human thought.' Music, like sixth sense, is typically a 'punter's hunch' that helps even scientists in their research. According to Hoene Wronski, a Polish philosopher, 'Music is the corporealization of the intelligence that is in sound.'

How music can affect the memory of an individual is very intriguing. Music by Beethoven or Mozart, with, say, 60 beats per minute pattern, can activate both the left and the right brain simultaneously. This maximizes the learning potential and retention of information. The information being studied activates the left brain while the right brain is activated by the musical inputs. The brain becomes more capable of processing information because of such an activity that engages both sides of the brain.

Another facet of music is that one may forget the words of a song but rarely does one forget its rhythm. The moment you get an external cue for a song that you may have heard almost a decade ago, you would be able to hum its tune, even if you cannot recollect its lyrics.

Creating icons, creating plots

Creating new characters is another aspect of imagination. How did someone first think of a Superman or a Batman or a Phantom? These characters were described in so much detail that they became life-like, indeed larger than life. Movies made on Superman and Spiderman earned and entertained millions. But actually they were nothing more than figments of imagination. Similar is the case of James Bond.

Plots and stories have been created around these characters. To create an intriguing plot requires an imaginative mastermind. Even engineering drawing—making of three-dimensional drawings on paper—requires great imaginative skill. You need to understand and portray in your mind what exists 'behind' the figure that you are looking at.

Imagining in the Scientific Domain

> *'Knowledge is limited, imagination encircles the world.'*
> —Albert Einstein

Albert Einstein was a physicist, scientist and explorer. His contribution to physics in particular, and science in general, remains unsurpassed even today. His scope of work was so huge that it remains mindboggling, not only for ordinary men but also for the entire scientific community.

His understanding of the atom and subatomic particles exhibited the micro side of his understanding God's creation. On the macro side, he looked at the vast galaxies, the mysterious black hole and the universe itself. He talked about the unfathomable—the frontiers of human understanding, of our living space and of the entire universe. Where was the end of space or the edge of space, and what would be beyond that? He closely examined time and its nature vis-á-vis light. He saw energy in matter, massive energy. He showed how matter could be converted into energy.

He demonstrated to the world the power of nature through science, the enormity of space and time, in front of which we become insignificant. There was a notion of the infinite and the finite in his ideas. He said, 'When I examine myself and my methods of thought, I come to the conclusion that the gift of fantasy has meant more to me than my talent for absorbing positive knowledge.' His insights did not come from logic or mathematics alone. He thought and imagined like a creative artist. His ideas were as much inspired and intuitive as mathematical and thought-out. He once said, 'All great achievements of science must start from intuitive knowledge. At times I feel certain that I am right while not knowing the reason.'

In 1929, when a journalist interviewed him in Berlin, Einstein was asked, 'Do you attribute your discoveries to intuition or inspiration?' He replied, 'I feel both; I sometimes feel right but do not know it. But when scientists went to test my theory, I was convinced that they would confirm my theory. I was not surprised by this but would have been surprised had I been wrong.'

Einstein imagined differently

During his visit to Japan in 1922, for a conference at Kyoto, Einstein mentioned that he used 'images' to solve problems, and found the connecting words later. He further said that he always thought in musical architectures, even in inner feelings, and did not think in terms of mathematical equations. He also said that no scientist thought in equations. After his first step of imagery was successful, he would take the next step of translating it into words.

While attributing his theories to imagination and music he said, 'If I were not a physicist, I would probably be a musician and I get most joy in music.' His son also recalled that whenever Einstein was stuck with a problem, he would take refuge in music. He would come out of his study and play the violin or piano and after a while say, 'There now, I got it', and move back to the study room as if the music had given him a solution.

'If you want your children to be intelligent, read them fairy tales. If you want them to be more intelligent, read them more fairy tales.'
—Albert Einstein

LESSONS FROM THE LIFE OF AN INNOVATIVE GENIUS

1. Imagination is mankind's biggest strength. It outweighs IQ and EI.
2. You can improve your ability to imagine. There are some simple ways to fire your imagination, which can be practised and made into a habit.
3. Imagination is the seed of invention and creativity.

6

NURTURE ALLIED TALENTS

All Work and No Play Makes Jack a Dull Boy

'A hobby a day keeps the doldrums away.'
—Phyllis McGinley

Life can become very boring if we have no other interests than our work. God has given each one of us a gift or two, which we can nurture as hobbies. Such hobbies, most importantly, act like soothers and help smoothen the rough edges of our daily routine. They also help us pass time even when we feel lonely.

As a bonus, these hobbies make our minds more agile, help us improve our imagination and boost our thinking process. Hobbies also trigger new ideas, because while we are enjoying what we love to do our mind is very calm and quiet, which gives rise to new ideas. Last, but not the least, we can also find our role models while pursuing our hobby.

There is one rule, though: don't copy others. If your friend is taking cooking classes or is going for dancing or singing lessons, do not follow him or her blindly. First, try things out to identify what you like. You must continue only if it makes sense to you, otherwise a hobby will become a punishment and its very purpose would be defeated.

And don't convince yourself that you are too busy and therefore you have no time to nurture or pursue a hobby. Albert Einstein had his hands full with his research, lecture tours, philanthropy and social activism, but he still found time for his hobbies. He loved playing his violin and piano. He also loved sailing and spending time with his pets. If he could find time, why can't you?

Einstein's Love for Music

Einstein's mother Pauline was pretty accomplished at playing the piano. His parents, especially his mother, wanted him to learn music and thus put him through violin lessons at the tender age of six. One has to appreciate that the violin is one of the most difficult musical instruments to play, and it takes a lot of patience to learn even the basics. Therefore, initially he was not comfortable with it and didn't really enjoy it. He started liking music only when he heard compositions by Mozart at the age of thirteen. At seventeen, he played at a musical examination in school and was appreciated by his teachers.

From 1902 to 1909, when Einstein worked in the patent office and was also doing research on his own, he spent time listening to Mozart. From then on, music was not just a pastime but the soul of his creative life.

He admired Beethoven but revered Mozart. According to him, Beethoven created his music, but Mozart simply plucked out music from the universe; music which was already created by nature, waiting to be picked up by someone as great as

Mozart. Einstein too, like Mozart, had meagre resources. He was living in a small shanty-like apartment when he discovered his spectacular theories in 1905. He identified his struggles with that of Mozart's. He believed that there was a lot of similarity between how Mozart picked the music out of the universe and how he picked up the laws of physics, which were nothing but the laws of nature. He felt that he had simply plucked the law of relativity from the cosmos as it was there, waiting to be discovered by someone who could understand it. For him it was more thought-driven rather than based on any calculation or numbers. Mozart's classical music inspired romantic music for future generations. Similarly, Einstein, through his theories, provided the foundation for atomic physics and scientific progress that was to take place in the next hundred years.

Einstein played music from his heart, right from his childhood. Though he never became a great violinist, his school friends noticed that sometimes when he played the violin, it was as if Mozart himself was playing. Yes, this is what people said! Note that it was only 'sometimes' that he showed his genius as a musician. In his later days, he performed at musical evenings and enjoyed playing in front of a cheering audience. Ladies, especially, loved him for this. Einstein also played the piano and was able to improvise some of his own music. His second wife, Elsa, fell in love with him as a little girl because he played Mozart so beautifully on the violin. In her later years, she also said that very often, when he got stuck with any problem related to his research at home, he would walk out of his study, play the piano or violin for a while, jot down some notes and resume his work as if he had found a solution.

Einstein recognized music as one of his important creative faculties. He said, 'Life without music is inconceivable for me; I live my daydreams in music. I see my life in terms of music and I get most joy in life only from my music.' He never travelled anywhere without his violin.

For him music was a great stimulator. It not only made him relax but also brought out the genius in him. He himself believed and admitted that his creativity and heightened sense of understanding of the complexities of his discoveries was because of his ability to play the violin.

Though he mostly played for his own pleasure, he also played with established musicians of his time like Fritz Kreisler and pianist Artur Schnabel. He also got along well with scientists of his time like Max Planck and sometimes even played with him.

As Einstein became famous and acquired a celebrity status, he was invited to play at charity concerts, which he eagerly accepted. He loved to play in orchestras as well.

'Music doesn't lie. If there is something to be changed in this world, then it can only happen through music.'

—Jimi Hendrix

Einstein's Love for Sailing

Though Einstein was not very fond of sports, he loved to go out sailing. He was never scared, despite the fact that he didn't know how to swim!

Once in 1944, while sailing, his boat capsized when it hit a rock. Einstein was trapped under the sail and a rope entangled around his leg. Without panicking, he managed to come up to the surface of the water and was saved by a motorboat which was passing by.

He found sailing relaxing and often carried a paper, pencil

and his smoking pipe along so that he could do his work in a serene place.

His favourite sailing spot was the Nassau Point, Long Island, New York. This place is also historically important, as it was here that Einstein signed the famous letter to President F.D. Roosevelt that eventually led to the invention of the atom bomb. Every summer, he would take up a cottage at Nassau Point and sailed there regularly. His boat capsized many times and he had to be rescued by the locals of that area. He had an unimpressive dingy sailboat which he named *Tinef*, which in Hebrew means 'worthless junk'.

Einstein's Love for Animals

'The only escape from the miseries of life is music and cats...'
—Albert Schweitzer

Einstein loved his dog, Chico, who was his constant companion. He loved cats as well. He kept a large number of cats in his study room. He also had a tomcat named Tiger at one point. This cat was scared of the rain. Einstein, just to sympathize with his cat, used to say, 'I know what is wrong, but I don't know how to turn it off.'

Charles Dickens, another genius, once fondly said about animals: 'What greater gift than the love of a cat?'

Importance of Liberal Arts in Sharpening Our Minds

Liberal arts' education encompasses a wide variety of subjects covering literature, performing arts, music, history and philosophy, which is distinct from science, technology and management.

In the earlier days, liberal arts were considered essential for a citizen to take active part in civic life and also effectively contribute to society. In the modern context, where technology and management studies have become preferred choices because these provide better career options, humanities and liberal arts have taken a back seat.

If one looks at the profile of a management graduate or a hardcore technologist, it would be evident that humanities and liberal arts are completely missing from their curriculum. Science and management are more logic-driven whereas humanities deals with the softer side of the intellect. Therefore, those who do not have any exposure to liberal arts fail to develop their softer intellect, which is important for an individual's overall competence.

Albert Einstein learnt music and found it to be his 'comforting companion'. Playing the piano or violin was not only a liberating experience for him but it also invoked those 'intellectual triggers' in the scientific domain which were essential for his creative thinking. To ensure that our intellect develops to the fullest, liberal arts and associated subjects must become part and parcel of our life. Most of these can be taken up as a hobby. For instance, learning a foreign language may not help you get a job, but many people study foreign languages, just for fun.

The life and methods of Einstein teach us that regardless of one's domain expertise, every individual must devote a reasonable amount of time to pick up something from the liberal arts' domain.

'Note too that a faithful study of the liberal arts humanizes character and permits it not to be cruel.'
—Ovid

LESSONS FROM THE LIFE OF AN INNOVATIVE GENIUS

1. One must develop one or two hobbies. They help in reducing stress and are a good way to pass one's time.
2. It is important for every individual to pick up and pursue a few areas of interest from the liberal arts' domain. It helps in augmenting our overall intellectual capability.
3. Outdoor games are not only a source of fun and entertainment but also keep us physically fit. It is not necessary to excel at a particular sport; it should be played for enjoyment.

7

DEVELOP A SENSE OF HUMOUR

Laughter Is the Best Medicine

'When a man sits with a pretty girl for an hour it seems like a minute.
But let him sit on a hot stove for a minute and it is longer
than an hour. That's relativity.'
—Albert Einstein

People who have a smile on their faces are liked by everyone. Studies have also shown that if, during an interview, the interviewee smiles a few times, he or she would have a better chance of getting selected. People who have a humourous disposition are liked by their peers, their bosses and definitely their subordinates. Humour is something that can be cleverly used during serious meetings or discussions to wriggle out of a heated argument. During a presentation or while conducting a training session, one can crack a joke or pass a comment (without hurting anyone) which can make people laugh; this fetches some attention every speaker looks for. And, as they say, 'It doesn't cost you to smile.' A smile thus gets returns with no investment.

Having a sense of humour does not mean you go on cracking

jokes the whole day. Wit and humour work well when they are employed in a subtle way. One definition of wit is: 'A form of intelligent humour; the ability to say or write things that are clever and usually funny.' Clean humour and wit are things that do not descend into sarcasm or become demeaning. In simple words, humour should never hit below the belt. If this happens, it becomes a big negative in our relationship with others.

Inventing Humour Is an Art

It requires a very intelligent mind to crack a joke. People who can create one-liners are the ones who are also very intelligent. They can quickly invent humour and respond originally to any comment or question on the spur of the moment. Einstein had wit and humour in abundance. His quotes are in hundreds, each better than the other. Most of his quotes sparkle with wit and humour. Because of his sense of humour, he was a very likeable person. His colleagues and students loved this habit of Einstein.

See the lighter side of life

Einstein's sense of humour was infectious and rubbed off on the people who were in close touch with him. According to a story, having spent time with Einstein, his driver had also become very witty and could invoke intelligent humour. He used to accompany his employer and having listened to his lectures again and again, he became conversant with them. One day, this driver mentioned to Einstein that since he had heard Einstein's lectures so many times, he would probably be able to give a lecture on his behalf. Einstein was ready to experiment and when he was scheduled to give a lecture to an audience where nobody recognized him, he asked his driver to pose as Einstein and deliver the lecture, while he himself sat back and enjoyed the show.

The driver delivered a flawless lecture but was asked a difficult question at the end by a smart member of the audience. Unfazed, he retorted, 'The answer to that question is so simple that even my driver, sitting at the back, will be able to answer it.' And Einstein, who was sitting at the back posing as the driver, answered the question.

It is difficult to imagine that a person like Einstein, who had such serious and philosophical views about religion, God, the meaning of life and human existence, also had a lighter side to him. He knew how to laugh at himself and his shortcomings.

Learn to laugh at your shortcomings

Though a great scientist, Einstein was very poor at remembering names, phone numbers, dates and addresses. He once forgot his own address while returning home in a taxi. He asked the taxi driver, 'Do you know where Einstein lives?' The driver, who did not recognize him, said, 'Yes, everybody knows where he lives. Should I take you there?' Einstein agreed. Once there, Einstein revealed his identity to the driver, who was so overwhelmed that he didn't even charge him the fare.

Humour is infectious

If you are humorous, it affects those in your company. It brings a sparkle at the workplace and with time, others around you also start quipping; and that further adds to the warmth and bonhomie.

Some famous people with a great sense of humour

Mughal Emperor Akbar's favourite minister Birbal was known for his wit and humour. He could respond to a situation with a witty retort at the spur of the moment and was therefore famous for being a 'haazir jawaab' which roughly translates into 'a person who can come up with a clever answer instantly'. With his metaphoric aptitude, it is said he could solve complex problems for Emperor Akbar through wit and humour. Tales of Akbar and Birbal's humorous exchanges are part of Indian folklore.

Richard Feynman, a Nobel Prize winner, had a great sense of humour. He also played musical instruments, was keen on art as well as something as unusual as lock-picking. George Clooney and Tom Hanks are not just brilliant actors, they also have a great sense of humour. Ronald Reagan, the former president of America, had a good sense of humour. In India, Lalu Prasad Yadav also has a good sense of humour and is quite witty. Prime Minister Narendra Modi also has the knack of injecting humorous asides in serious speeches, to engage his audience.

Connection between humour, intelligence and creativity

When we laugh at a joke, we do so because of its incongruities or due to something in it that does not meet conventional expectations. Jokes provide a different perspective from our normal way of looking at things.

If you come to think of it, the essence of lateral thinking or out-of-the-box thinking is to break away from routine, and disregard conventional expectations. Einstein was unconventional; that is why he imagined himself running along a beam of light.

Cracking a joke or even understanding one requires lateral thinking because your mind has to travel in an unconventional direction to understand it. What is unconventional sounds stupid and what is stupid is a joke.

Consider this: 'Two aerials get married. The ceremony was rubbish but the reception was brilliant.' It requires some intelligence to understand this because it is unconventional. It is not surprising when someone says, 'He is such a dope that he can't even understand a joke!'

Here's another: a man goes to the doctor and says, 'Have you got anything for wind?' The doctor gives him a kite!

Humour is a universal aspect of human psychology, as language and race have no bar on it. Several studies have been carried out to determine the correlation between humour and intelligence.

W.E. Hanck and J.W. Thomas once carried out a study to find out the relationship between humour and intelligence and creativity. They concluded that creativity and intelligence were independent but a sense of humour correlated highly with both.

Another study was conducted by MacDonald and Howrigan where they studied a group of college students to determine any correlation between intelligence and humour. They found that intelligence was a predictor of humour. They also established that humour is an indicator of mental fitness.

How to develop a sense of humour

If nothing else, humour brings joy and happiness to our lives. Einstein, like many others, was born with a humorous disposition. But those who are not as lucky can also make efforts to bring humour into their lives such as:

- Make friends with people who have a good sense of humour. It is infectious and as you spend more time with them, laughter will become a part of your life.
- Watch light-hearted comedy shows and movies. It can give you ideas on how to make humour a part of your life.
- Read funny books or joke books.
- Use social media to share jokes with your friends.
- Learn to laugh at yourself.
- Look at the funny side of life. Try and shrug off an embarrassing situation with laughter.

'A man who can drive safely while kissing a pretty girl is simply not giving the kiss the attention it deserves.'

—Albert Einstein

LESSONS FROM THE LIFE OF AN INNOVATIVE GENIUS

1. Humour is the lighter side of life, which brings joy to everyone.
2. It is good to have friends who have a sense of humour as they make life more enjoyable.
3. If you have a humorous disposition, people will get attracted to you. Indirectly, it can also help in networking.

8

THINK SMART

Make Your Mind More Agile and Productive

'Everybody is a genius. But if you judge a fish by its ability to climb a tree, it will live its whole life believing that it is stupid.'
—Albert Einstein

Albert Einstein was not only intelligent in the conventional sense of the term (he had one of the highest-recorded IQs), but he also magnified the impact of his IQ by his ability to simplify things and articulate his ideas with wit and humour. This is something we need to learn from this brilliant scientist. He also had that raw practical sense of what was good and what was bad, and was, in his own way, pretty street-smart. He further augmented his potential by getting involved in different and diverse areas of scientific research. He was always willing to experiment with scientific projects, even if they were not related to his fundamental fields of expertise. Scientists of his time, and the world, believed that he had a brain which was better than the rest of us because he had a very high IQ as well as great imaginative skills.

Importance of IQ

Alfred Binet, a French psychologist, was the founding father of the concept of Intelligence Quotient or IQ. The first formal IQ test was created by him and his research assistant Théodore Simon in 1905. It was known as the Binet-Simon test. Binet was fascinated by brilliant chess players and often wondered how some of them could play multiple games simultaneously. This became the starting point for his investigation into human intelligence.

Those were the days of the Industrial Revolution and society's progress largely depended on inventions and discoveries related to physics, chemistry, mathematics and biology. Therefore, logical reasoning became the basis of assessing human competence. People who were good at these subjects were considered intelligent.

According to the Binet-Simon test, a person with average-level intelligence would score between 85–115. Just 1 per cent of the people in the world would have an IQ of more than 135. Those who scored more than 150 were supposed to be extraordinarily brilliant and God-gifted. Albert Einstein's IQ was 160, whereas world chess champion Bobby Fischer scored 187. Mozart had an IQ of 165. Several studies have been conducted to link IQ with genes and scientists have been able to identify a group of genes that are related to one's IQ.

A Genius All the Way

Einstein's name is synonymous with genius. When he died in 1955, his brain was removed before he was cremated and preserved for further studies. The scientists wanted to examine the differences between the brains of ordinary people and extraordinary men like Einstein. His brain was cut into about 240 slices and preserved and photographed from many angles.

The researchers did find some revealing differences and made some peculiar observations. First, he had an unusual brain anatomy; some parts of his brain were missing. This, they concluded, allowed neurons in the brain to communicate more effectively and that is why Einstein thought the way he did.

It was also observed that the two hemispheres of his brain had better connections than in the case of other people of his age. His remarkable ability to conceptualize ideas and 'think visually' was attributed to the unusual patterns of grooves and ridges not found in other people.

Communication Skills and Articulation

When we speak, three things count. First, how we speak, which is basically related to our diction, accent and pronunciation. Second, what we speak, which means the content or the next part of the communication process. If we don't prepare, make notes or do our research on the subject, we will fumble with facts. The third is how we logically structure our thoughts and how we use analogies to explain our point. This is what is known as the art of articulation. I have seen people with good accents do a lot of homework to build content, but they are unable to explain their point to the audience. They simply lack clarity and logical thought process. It is all about how you structure your content and thoughts and then make your ideas flow in a logical manner, such that the audience can get it right straightaway. I have seen brilliant engineers unable to sell an idea just because of their lack of 'thought clarity'. Many a time if we have too much content, we complicate the issue beyond comprehension.

Albert Einstein had the ability to put his ideas across in the most logical way. He also had the knack of simplifying things. He learnt to articulate his views at the patent office because he had to evaluate several patent applications every day. In those days, a patent application described the object in detail and it was mandatory to produce a working model, which was to be reviewed by the patent clerk. Einstein used to give strict instructions to the inventors to explain briefly and clearly how their device worked. He preferred it if a person could express his or her point of view in just one sentence. He also learnt how to reach the core of the scientific basis of every invention.

Einstein was absolutely right when he said, 'If you can't explain it to a six-year-old, you don't understand it yourself.' So always make it simple. Add a dash of humour and you will be great.

> 'You see, wire telegraph is a kind of a very, very long cat. You pull his tail in New York and his head is meowing in Los Angeles. Do you understand this? And radio operates exactly the same way: you send signals here, they receive them there. The only difference is that there is no cat.'

—Albert Einstein's way of explaining the difference between a wire line and a wireless communication system.

Analogy, Metaphor and Simile Are Great Ways to Enhance Your Communication

'The greatest thing by far is to be a master of metaphor.'
—Aristotle

Analogies between unlike ideas and objects, similes and metaphors can be very cleverly used to explain a point effectively.

'Her hair glistened in the rain like nose hair after a sneeze' or 'she walked onto the stage like a centipede with ninety-eight legs missing' are funny similes. The usual metaphors are like this: 'I was dog-tired after the exams'. Some famous quotes by Einstein were analogies or metaphors.

'Two things are infinite: the universe and human stupidity, and I am not sure about the universe' and 'Science without religion is lame, religion without science is blind' are two very effective quotes that connect unconnected things beautifully.

Diversify Your Portfolio to Make Your Mind More Agile

Never get stuck in a groove. In today's times when technological concepts become obsolete in less than three years, can you afford to remain behind others by not learning new things?

People nowadays have started going for courses in journalism and acting rather than management and engineering. Mathematicians have become motivational coaches and doctors now want to join the civil services. People who do not broaden their horizons may fail to exploit their potential. For example, actor John Abraham got his MBA degree from Narsee Monjee Institute of Management, whereas actor Preity Zinta holds a master's degree in criminal psychology. Similarly, even in the case of acting, actors try out different genres.

Einstein worked on very divergent subjects throughout his life. He dabbled in quantum mechanics and worked on photoelectric effect on the one hand and equally and intensely perused the theory of special and general relativity on the other. He gave the world the connection between matter and energy, which was the fundamental explanation of nuclear power and nuclear energy. He worked with Satyendra Nath Bose to come up with the Bose-Einstein statistical analysis at a highly microscopic level. He worked on a new type of refrigerator with a totally different principle from the technology available in those days.

From microscopic subatomic particles to the macroscopic universe and cosmos, Einstein worked on a diverse range of scientific scrutiny. He laid the foundation for modern cosmology and was always ahead of his times.

Become Worldly-wise

David Wechsler, a psychologist, defined human intelligence as: 'The global and aggregate capacity of the individual to think rationally, to act purposefully and to deal effectively with the environment.'

Contrary to the belief that scientists are weird, geeks or technical dopes, Albert Einstein, in spite of his casual, couldn't-care-less attitude, displayed a remarkable sense of judgement of the environment he lived in.

From 1925 onwards, as Hitler's Nazi Party was making rapid strides to take over Germany, Jews were feeling the heat of hatred. Many thought it to be a passing phase, and therefore stayed back in Germany, losing their lives at the hands of the Nazis in the bargain.

Einstein realized that Germany was not a safe place for him to live in as he was a Jew. They labelled his work as 'Jewish physics', rebuked him, raided his villa in Berlin and seized his books and bank accounts. He was worldly-wise enough to know what was coming. He spent a few years in England and did some teaching assignments before permanently migrating to America in 1933, i.e., before Hitler came to power.

Being worldly-wise and being able to decipher the tell-tale marks has nothing to do with one's IQ. It is a strong contender for being a part of emotional intelligence and is closely associated with social intelligence.

How to Improve Your IQ

There is no set formula to improve one's IQ but there are certainly some activities that can help in stimulating the brain. It is like mental gymnastics: 'use it or lose it'. Some of the activities that one should engage oneself in are:

- Playing games like chess, scrabble, Sudoku and doing crossword puzzles.
- Exercising regularly, as it releases good chemicals in the brain and helps the growth of brain cells through neurogenesis.
- Creating new things and getting involved in different projects.
- Breaking monotony and doing the same things differently. For instance, driving or cycling down to the same location using different routes.
- Exploring new locations, new hobbies and new people.
- Being inquisitive; curiosity absorbs knowledge.
- Observing and absorbing. Be observant and look at things carefully and examine them in the minutest details.
- Reading different subjects and trying to write a short summary of what one has read.
- Eating well. Fruits, fish and nuts help in building a healthy mind.
- Limiting TV viewing as too much TV makes one's mind dumb and inactive.

How to Become More Productive

Einstein's way of research and his working methodology teaches us several simple but important things that help us in becoming more productive.

- Have a goal that you care about. Think about it and keep yourself motivated.
- Thereafter, work hard to achieve this goal because there are no shortcuts.
- Follow your gut feeling; it is intuition or the sixth sense that helps you create new things.
- Spend a lot of time on your ideas. But have clarity of thought.
- Learn everything, but use what you need. Try to shed the excess baggage of ideas and keep them simple.
- Do not get discouraged by others—be bold. Listen to people but do what you feel is right.
- Progress usually comes from the least-expected quarters. Therefore, keep looking in all directions—you don't know where it might come from.

'Look deep into nature, and then you will understand everything better.'
—Albert Einstein

LESSONS FROM THE LIFE OF AN INNOVATIVE GENIUS

1. Even if one doesn't have a high IQ, it can be compensated for with hard work.
2. Articulation is an important part of communication skills.
3. Above all, one must be worldly-wise and street-smart to do well in life.

9

ACCEPT FAILURES AND SETBACKS

Life Is not a Bed of Roses

> *'Success consists of going from failure to failure without loss of enthusiasm.'*
> —Winston Churchill

Delayed Gratification and Willpower

For people who need to be individual performers like athletes, bodybuilders, musicians or even scientists, success is never instantaneous. It is a long, hard journey to success.

In the case of Albert Einstein too, willpower and perseverance paved the way to success. He was delving into areas of science which nobody had ever thought of. He was looking into the invisible world of electrons and atoms, the speed of light, the size of the universe and black holes. His theories would often be ripped apart by fellow scientists and many a time slammed by the media. He had to therefore work on each of his new ideas very patiently and move ahead step by step.

At the tipping point of his career, in 1905, Einstein wrote

four scientific papers that had far-reaching implications on modern physics. The expanse of his work included time, mass, energy and space—four major dimensions of our very existence. He was working at the patent office then, where he had little access to scientific literature and had very few fellow scientists to consult with. In order to achieve what he set out to do, he had to have a lot of patience and the will to wait for results.

A case in point is the discovery of photoelectric effect and light quanta, which he wrote about in one of his papers in 1905. It was initially rejected by the scientific community and contemporary giants like Neils Bohr and Max Planck. This discovery became universally accepted only in 1919 and he received a Nobel Prize for the same in 1921. He had to wait for sixteen long years for this reward.

He never lacked enthusiasm and therefore worked on several scientific discoveries and theories simultaneously. Throughout his career, he was trying to develop a unified field theory. He even published papers on the subject but could never succeed in coming up with an acceptable theory. He also left some unsuccessful investigations on subjects like superconductivity, gravitational waves and black holes. To receive bouquets of success along with many brickbats is not easy. It requires patience as well as self-motivation to survive under such circumstances.

Einstein had the courage to delve into diverse areas of science because he was never afraid of failure. He failed in several research works and projects that he attempted throughout his life. Failure never deterred him from his adventurous pursuit of discovering new things.

Works of many great authors are rejected several times before they are published. For instance, *Harry Potter and the Philosopher's Stone* by J.K. Rowling was rejected a dozen times by publishers before being published by Bloomsbury. When Joseph Heller sent out his manuscript of *Catch-22*, it was rejected and returned by a publisher who said: 'I haven't the foggiest idea about what the man is trying to say... Apparently, the author intends to be funny but it is not funny on any intellectual level.' Later, the book sold more than ten million copies and still is a bestseller. Remember, success, failure and rejections go hand in hand.

As the great Thomas Edison said, 'Many of life's failures are people who did not realize how close they were to success when they gave up.'

Cosmology

Cosmology is the science of studying the universe—how it all began, its origin and its growth or expansion, and possibly also the ultimate fate of the universe. This field has always intrigued the human race and its study has been in existence for the past four to five thousand years. As per recorded history, Hindu cosmology is the oldest and describes the universe to be infinite and ever-existing. More scientific analysis was done by Sir Isaac Newton in 1670, and he proposed that every particle or body in the universe attracts every other particle or body to maintain a gravitational balance.

Albert Einstein gave cosmology a different perspective by applying his theory of relativity to cosmos and cosmic existence. He created an expanding universe which was finite but unbounded. He came up with a term, 'cosmological constant', to describe the universe as a static entity. He abandoned this theory and called it his greatest blunder after Edwin Hubble, in 1929, discovered that the universe is not static but expanding.

Study of the cosmos is a very complex process. Einstein may not have contributed a lot towards cosmology, but he had definitely dabbled in this problem and applied his mind to something that has intrigued mankind for centuries.

Einstein was always ready to get involved in any project, even if it was not directly related to his field. It is difficult to imagine a Nobel laureate and a scientist of his calibre getting involved in making a refrigerator. But he always looked for new opportunities.

His motivation to invent something different came from the fact that refrigerators in those days were prone to malfunctions, which could end up as an accident. There were cases where toxic fumes had accidently leaked and caused deaths.

Einstein's model of the refrigerator used gas as a refrigerant and required only a heat source like a stove or solar energy to work. He got a patent for it in 1930. Since the conventional models became more effective and safe, the Einstein refrigerator was never really manufactured at a commercial level and consequently never achieved commercial success. Such a failed invention would have discouraged many others, but for Einstein it was just another research project.

Unified Field Theory

In scientific terms, a field is an area that is under the effect, spell or influence of some force, like gravitational pull or a magnet. The theory of electromagnetism was the first field theory proposed by James Maxwell. The entire radio communication was built on Maxwell's equations as well. Einstein's general theory of relativity was the next field theory dealing with gravitation. Later, Einstein wanted to integrate every theory into his unified field theory, which was to demonstrate that electromagnetism and gravitational field are two different manifestations of the same fundamental field.

This is still open for research since Einstein, even in his last few years, could not conclude this research.

'Anyone who has never made a mistake has never tried anything new.'
—Albert Einstein

LESSONS FROM THE LIFE OF AN INNOVATIVE GENIUS

1. Strong willpower and the ability to work hard and be patient are the mantras for success.
2. Einstein, a Nobel laureate, too, had to taste failure many times in life. Failures should not deter you from your course of action.
3. Always look for opportunities and challenges.

10

DISRUPTIVE THINKING

Practise Inventive Leadership

'Our wretched species is so made that those who walk on the well-trodden path always throw stones at those who are showing a new road.'
—Voltaire

What Is Disruptive Thinking?

If one has to go by the books, 'disrupt' means to throw into turmoil or disorder. Therefore, anything related to disruption implies upsetting, unruly or tumultuous. In a more positive sense, it means breaking away from the status quo or challenging what already exists.

Though today management gurus call this something new and path-breaking, a disruptive way of thinking is something that existed all along.

Nicolaus Copernicus, in 1543, put forth the idea that the sun was at the centre of the universe and the earth (rotating on its own axis) orbited around the sun. It was a challenge to the commonly held beliefs, backed even by the church, that all stars including the sun revolve around a stationary earth. Much later, in 1610, Galileo Galilei used his first basic telescope to observe other planets more clearly and prove what Copernicus had put forth. It is nothing but disruptive thinking which challenges the very core of any existing norm or belief.

When authors come up with titles of their books like *The World Is Flat* (2005) by Thomas Friedman they again force you to look at something that appears out of the ordinary. Friedman, in his book, demonstrates that the world is now interconnected and hence has trigged the globalization process, providing a level playing field to all those who wish to do business across the globe.

How can a monk sell a Ferrari? First of all, how on earth can a monk own a Ferrari? This thought gave a disruptive name to a book, *The Monk Who Sold His Ferrari* (1997). People liked this title because it challenged their very belief.

In his book *Disrupt* (2010), Luke Williams compares product differentiators with outright disruptive thinking. He argues that in the service sector or even in the manufacturing industry, the emphasis is to make the same product different by working around it and trying to play with certain parameters of the existing product. A car can be manufactured as a hatchback, a tall boy model or it can have curved headlights—there is no radical change in this process.

This happens because people like to remain in their comfort zone, secure in what has been accepted over a period of time. They love the status quo. They are ready to make incremental changes, but are not ready to take on that which they feel is not right for them. Status quo, in fact, is the death of invention.

Coming up with something new, where you are the only one who does what you do, is at the heart of invention and innovation. When Henry Ford was working on a petrol engine, people thought he was crazy. Many asked him not to waste his time and divert his energy towards electrical energy instead as at that point, electricity was the most talked-about discovery. Imagine if he had stayed with the status quo, there would have been no automobile industry.

Disruptive thinking is what takes an industry or a business to a different level, or even the next generation.

For instance, the computer transited from small to mini to mainframes and then went on to transform into micros, laptops and palmtops. We also have large super computers. But they all work on logic gates and information is stored, handled and processed in a binary format. A bit is either a 0 or a 1. A combination of three bits would give 2^3 or eight fixed combinations.

Quantum computers are a new revolution in the computing world and are being researched everywhere. Here the information will be stored in 'qubits or quantum bits'. A single qubit could represent a 0 or a 1 or it could be in a super position of these two states. Therefore, 'n' qubits in a string can be in any arbitrary superposition of up to 2^n states simultaneously, unlike a conventional computer that can be only in one fixed deterministic state.

This is disruptive innovation, which can make computers enormously powerful and they can be deployed for cryptology, medicine and artificial intelligence. These machines can solve mathematical problems which conventional computers would take centuries to solve.

In short, disruptive thinking is thinking the unthinkable. With technology at its peak, this is the best time for experimenting with disruptive thought processes. For instance, the Internet coupled with new-age telecom has given rise to new industries. E-learning, e-commerce and e-marketing are some of the new innovations, which can be called a paradigm shift in business models. Imagine, Facebook with a market cap of over US$70 billion, does not have any factory!

Albert Einstein was way ahead of his times. He thought of the unthinkable. Luke Williams says: 'Be wrong at the start to be right at the end.' Therefore, think what no one else is thinking and do what no one else is doing. It is like a maverick at work. It all starts with the wackiest thoughts or some wild questions like: 'What if?'

'Warren Buffet told me once and he said always follow your gut. When you have that gut feeling, you have to go with don't go back on it.'
—LeBron James, American professional basketball player

Einstein Was a Disruptive Thinker

Einstein thought differently and expressed his opinions very candidly with subtle expressions that were too good to be ignored. To express his views on the negative impact of scientific progress he once said, 'Technological progress is like an axe in the hands of a pathological criminal.'

Einstein was not a conformist and always challenged the status quo. He changed the rules of the game in most of the areas that he worked on. As explained earlier, he shattered the myth of 'absolute' and brought about a view of the universe where space and time were dependent on the frames of reference. Everything can be viewed as being relative to another. For example, there are two mountains, one which is 25,000 feet high and the other 20,000 feet high; they are both very tall individually but in comparison, one is taller than the other by only 5,000 feet. This is the change which his idea of relativity brought in our everyday social order, our morals and even our duty. Though not directly, the theory of relativity was associated with relativism in morality, politics and art and literature. It helped break the imaginative conformity of the absolute, and thinkers started breaking conventional bonds, be it Pablo Picasso, Igor Stravinsky or Sigmund Freud. They created a whole new environment of opinion under which people debated. His aggressive thinking therefore impacted not only the field of science and technology but also the cultural side of human existence.

Intuition and the Sixth Sense

Intelligence, as defined by IQ, is intelligence from the head, whereas emotional intelligence is from the heart and to an extent from the gut. Intuition is like a hunch, a gut feeling; and hence it partially belongs to the EI domain and to a large extent to what is now believed to be spiritual intelligence. It is something that lies between the spirit and the heart. We have five senses, according to which we perceive the worldly things or the physical realm we live in. As a corollary to this, since the five senses can perceive reality, they cannot discern what goes on in the 'unseen realm'. To see the unseen, we depend on intuition, or the sixth sense. For most people, hunches, gut feelings and sixth sense seem to be cryptic, abstract or even enigmatic.

Rumi, a thirteenth-century Sufi mystic and poet has said, 'Your task? To work with all your passion of your being to acquire an inner light.'

From light to photons, the universe, matter, black holes and the cosmos, Einstein had his plate full. Understanding the cosmos and our very existence can be related to spirituality. Sixth sense, therefore, is also known as extrasensory perception (ESP) and is synonymous to clairvoyance and even premonition. It is not difficult to imagine that Einstein relied on his intuition or sixth sense to see what was actually not visible to the naked eye.

To some extent, we all have a sixth sense. That is why many of us get those intuitional nudges at times. Sometimes these get drowned by our five physical senses and on other occasions we simply ignore them.

To enhance one's sixth sense, one has to use it as much as one can. It is like invoking your second sight. Sages, saints and monks utilized their sixth sense to get answers to complex problems. Meditation is the breeding ground for these 'insight triggers'.

Though each one of us possesses intuitive ability to some extent, scientific enlightenment dawns upon only a few of us. Albert Einstein was probably one of those gifted scientists who could amalgamate logical reasoning with intuition and willfully connect it to the spiritual angle whenever required. His interpretation of the complexity and ever-expanding nature of our universe could not have been churned out of an ordinary mind. It had to be a gift of God, which few have and fewer are able to cultivate.

Einstein admitted that he depended upon his sixth sense. He worked with science, theorized the laws of nature, got intimate with the mystery of our existence and flirted with time and space. It left him in awe, humbled him and made him look at God and religion differently.

He once said, 'Every scientist becomes convinced that a spirit is manifest in the laws of the universe; a spirit vastly superior to that of man and we with our modest powers must feel humble. It leads to a religious feeling which is quite different from religiosity of someone more naïve.' He therefore rejected the idea of a personal god and looked at God as a being who reveals Himself in the harmony of all that exists.

A man who had so much 'freedom and creativity' was humbled by the expanse and order of our vast cosmos and therefore proclaimed that he was a determinist—'a person bound by the doctrine that every event is the inevitable consequence of antecedent state of affairs.' A human ultimately cannot have freedom of choice because it violates the law of cosmic causality, and that is why he once said: 'God does not play dice with the universe.'

How to Become a Disruptive Thinker?

'One has to passionately believe that it is possible to change the industry, to turn it on its head, to make sure that it will never be the same again.'
—Richard Branson

Addressing the corporate and the business world, Luke Williams in his book has explained a step-by-step strategy to come up with disruptive ideas.

- Craft your disruptive hypothesis.
- Come up with something radically new; it may be weird or even wrong to start with.
- Explore the unexpected areas of your business environment. Look at the gaps that exist, and look where no one is looking. These are your best disruptive opportunities.

- Then give it a shape, a meaning and description. Don't create mundane stuff just for the sake of creating something.
- Make your winning disruptive pitch by over-preparing and over-emphasizing the unusual but underplaying the obvious routine stuff.

Disruptive thinking is similar to chaotic thinking with some filters to manage the chaotic mind and come up with something radically different. Sometimes it is as simple as common sense. Therefore, use your common sense.

Leadership is all about disruptive ideas and common sense. Look at India's current prime minister, Shri Narendra Modi. He comes up with great ideas which are simple, different and workable. He challenges the status quo. He came up with a solar power project which envisaged solar panels to be installed across 19,000 kilometres of the Narmada canal network. He has also initiated a pilot project in April 2014 to generate 1.6 million units of clean energy per annum and to also prevent 9 million litres of canal water from evaporating every year. You can call it out-of-the-box thinking, lateral thinking, ambidextrous thinking or maverick thinking; they all challenge the status quo.

While it is possible to learn how to think disruptively, it may not be possible to trigger intuition at will. Carl Jung, a psychotherapist, defined intuition as 'Perception via the unconscious', and further said that an intuitive and attentive mind worked and acted on sheer intensity of perception. Such a mind keeps chasing new ideas, even if the old ones have not been fully matured. People with such minds are in constant pursuit of change. This is a grey area in the realm of psychology as well as science. It is difficult to come to a conclusion regarding intuitive thinking because on the one hand it depends on the sheer intensity of thought and perception, while on the other it could be triggered by the unconscious mind.

'The only real valuable thing is intuition.'
—Albert Einstein

LESSONS FROM THE LIFE OF AN INNOVATIVE GENIUS

1. Keep your mind open to new ideas.
2. Be prepared to be different and challenge the status quo. You never know what is in store for you when you come up with whacky ideas.
3. Today, technology is at its best. We are living in an age of opportunities. The only thing that limits opportunities is our limited imagination.
4. If you get a weird idea, it could be a gut feeling or intuition. Don't suppress it, listen to that intuition and act on it.
5. We all get ideas, but those who preserve these ideas and act on them become successful. The most practical way of perceiving these 'thought triggers' is to write them down immediately because they appear rapidly and also disappear as quickly. You can jot these down on a paper or store them on your mobile phone. Later, you can look at these at leisure.

11

COURAGE OF CONVICTION

Belief, Integrity, Solidarity, Honesty

*'Don't allow your mind to tell your heart what to do.
The mind gives up easily.'*
—Paulo Coelho

According to the dictionary, courage of one's convictions would mean, 'To do or say what you think is right; no matter who disagrees with you.' It is probably one of the key virtues of a good character. It may sound simple, but it is very difficult to have the courage of doing what 'you' think is right. In a broader sense, this quality acts like an inner compass for an individual. It defines the thin red line or 'Lakshman Rekha' for an individual that says, 'This far and no more', as far as one's morals and beliefs are concerned.

Your convictions are those beliefs that you are fully convinced about. Once you are convinced about something, your actions are defined accordingly. A cluster of such beliefs becomes your value system that determines your code of conduct, according to which you live your life. Thomas Carlyle, a Scottish philosopher, has rightly said, 'Conviction is worthless unless it is converted into conduct.'

It is therefore very important for each one of us to have a value system and it is equally important to live by it. Our upbringing, to a large extent, has a great influence in formulating our beliefs in what we think is right or wrong. As we grow up and mature into adults, the value system comes from our own hearts, i.e., from within. Thereafter, one has to have the courage to follow one's own value system. Not only do saints and soldiers have ethics and value systems, thieves, thugs and even dacoits have a code of conduct, even though it may be a perverted system of values.

The Sicilian Mafia, a criminal syndicate in Italy, is a collection of criminal groups that share a common code of conduct. Their members call themselves 'men of honour', though the public and the government call them criminals and mercenaries.

Sticking His Neck Out

> *'You have enemies? Good. That means you've stood up for something, sometime in your life.'*
> —Winston Churchill

For an honest man living within the precincts of law and the diktats of society, it requires tremendous courage to live by his convictions. In many cases and under certain circumstances it means sticking one's neck out, and sometimes even being prepared to put one's neck in the noose.

Albert Einstein, though an intellectual, academic and scientist, had enough courage to stand by his principles and speak his mind, even if it could go against him. When he was in school, he was not convinced about the method of teaching used there. He told his father about it and was prepared to migrate to any other country to get meaningful education. Later, in 1921, he strongly advocated that a school day should not be longer than six hours, and recommended that exams were not necessary to evaluate students. Thereafter, throughout his life, he stood up to what he felt was 'not right', according to him.

Einstein's Opposition to War

Einstein was against war since the very beginning. When the war sentiment was brewing in Germany, the Nazi Party was rallying the Germans to go for an all-out war. Einstein spoke against war while all other scientists, even those as respected as Max Planck, joined together to sign a manifesto endorsing Germany's war intentions as a justifiable action to stop Russians from invading. Only three scientists including Einstein opposed it. One of them was jailed, though Einstein was not, because of his celebrity status. Unfortunately, in January 1945, Max Planck's son Erwin was executed by the Gestapo for participating in the failed attempt to assassinate Hitler in July 1944.

Albert Einstein was against joining the army when it was being made a compulsory service before the war. He did not want to be party to it because he was against war and was convinced that war brought only misery and destruction.

Against Nazi Ideology

During the time when Hitler was making rapid strides to come into power, his political cronies were unleashing terror on anyone who opposed him. They were selectively targeting the Jews, burning their books, seizing their bank accounts and destroying their homes. Jews were banned from any government jobs including teaching. Einstein, being a Jew and a celebrity, was directly targeted. He didn't abandon his homeland for as long as he could. It is only when he realized that he would be killed by the Nazis that he moved to America. The important lesson to learn from him is to have the ability to understand how far is too far. This is extremely important because it is better to live and fight rather than get killed without doing anything worthwhile. This is one major trait that defines EI. US Army General George Patton has said, 'I want you to remember that no poor dumb bastard ever won a war by dying for his country. He won it by making the other poor bastard die for his country.'

Scientific Gut Feeling and Conviction

Einstein was fond of mathematics and science and once told a reporter in America, 'When I was just twelve years old and learning elementary maths, I was thrilled to understand that it was possible to find out truth by reasoning alone. At that time I became convinced that we can understand even nature by looking at it mathematically.' This remained his inner compass for the rest of his life.

Strong Views and Noble Intentions

'It is curious that physical courage should be so common in the world and moral courage so rare.'

—Mark Twain

Albert Einstein was a man of impeccable integrity and displayed high moral courage. People in a position like his need not display physical courage but they should have moral courage to express their opinions about topics that others usually avoid talking about. Such people should also have the courage to take criticism. In an article 'What I Believe', which he wrote for a journal, Einstein said, 'The ideals which have guided me have been kindness, truth and beauty.'

In this regard, Winston Churchill has also said, 'Courage is what it takes to stand up and speak; courage is also what it takes to sit down and listen.'

During his course of research, Einstein had to accept many rejections as well as failures. Research work can become frustrating because of a low success-to-failure ratio. It requires high level of internal motivation to continue working in such a hostile environment and tremendous courage to take criticism from your own community.

He said, 'As long as I have any choice in the matter, I shall live only in a country where civil liberty, tolerance and equality of all citizens before the law prevails.' He had the courage to defy Hitler's diktats and refused to bend down to Nazi pressure tactics. He was courageous enough to leave Germany, his homeland, and go to a new country like the US to settle down. This move provided him the freedom of action and speech.

Research and Creation of Knowledge

Einstein was the one who founded the Hebrew University of Jerusalem. He toiled hard to raise funds for it and had a vision for this institution which was to build a first-rate teaching and research university, so that high-grade research could be done and Jews from all over the world could benefit. The American Jews, who had contributed to it in a big way, wanted the university to come up as only a teaching college so that their kith and kin could get jobs in the university. Einstein later realized that the board of governors was not working in the right direction. Therefore, he resigned from the academic council and as a member of the board of governors.

A Jewish State

Einstein was not in favour of the Jews having a conflict with the Arabs. He wanted a way in which Jews and Arabs could coexist in Palestine; he was against a separate Jewish state. When Palestinians started feeling the impact of Jewish immigrants encroaching on their land, they were compelled to fight back and resist this migration. Einstein advised the Jews: 'Should we be unable to find a way to honest cooperation and pacts with Arabs, then we shall have learnt nothing from our 2,000 years of suffering and will deserve our fate.' Despite his strong views on this issue, he was offered the presidency of Israel. It is important to understand that such high degree of courage adds to one's credibility in a big way.

Efforts to Ban Nuclear Weapons

After the twin bombings of Hiroshima and Nagasaki, Einstein made a number of appeals and efforts to stop manufacturing nuclear weapons. He made full use of his celebrity status to garner media attention around this so as to put pressure on the US as well as the USSR and make them understand the stupidity of creating a nuclear weapon pile.

Dislike of Praise

Einstein had acquired a cult status by 1921, especially after receiving a Nobel Prize. He was mentioned in newspapers all over the world. Though he never read or even cared about what was written about him, he got a lot of attention from the press. He disliked biographies and told his friend, 'In this way, one doesn't get spoilt by praise or depressed by blame.'

Great People, Great Convictions

There have been several great people who have displayed courage in their convictions. They have also displayed grace under pressure.

In his first speech to the House of Commons after becoming the prime minister of England, Winston Churchill, on 13 May 1940, gave a speech which required a lot of courage, something very few men can muster.

This was the time when Hitler had captured almost half of Europe and was making rapid strides to finish France with his blitzkrieg strategy. England was the only hope if Europe had to survive. The entire burden of war thus fell on Churchill who in his address to the nation said,

> We are in the preliminary stage of one of the greatest battles in history. As I said to others who have joined the government, I would say to the house: I have nothing to offer but blood, toil, tears and sweat. We have before us an ordeal of the most grievous kind. We have before us many long months of struggle and suffering. If you ask what is our aim. It is one word Victory at all costs.

Abraham Lincoln made a great speech during his senatorial campaign on 16 June 1858 where he did not mince words. At that time, slavery was one of the biggest issues. There were many who were against it and many who wanted it to continue. He wanted to convey that the country could not be divided on the issue of slavery and thus said,

> A house divided against itself cannot stand. I believe this government cannot endure, permanently, half slave and half free. I do not expect the Union to be dissolved—I do not expect the house to fall—but I do expect it will cease to be divided. It will become all one thing or all the other. Either the opponents of slavery will arrest the further spread of it, and place it where the public mind shall rest in the belief that it is in the course of ultimate extinction; or its advocates will push it forward, till it shall become lawful in all the States, old as well as new—North as well as South.

At the fifth Nobel Anniversary Dinner in New York on 10 December 1945, after World War II was won by the Allies, Albert Einstein in a speech on 'War is Won, but Peace is Not' said:

> The war is won, but peace is not. The great powers, united in fighting, are now divided over the peace settlements. The world was promised freedom from fear, but in fact fear has increased tremendously since the termination of the war. The world was promised freedom from want, but large parts of the world are faced with starvation while others are living in abundance. The nations were promised liberation and justice. But we have witnessed, and are witnessing even now, the sad spectacle of 'liberating' armies firing into populations who want their independence and social equality, and supporting in those countries, by force of arms, such parties and personalities as appear to be most suited to serve vested interests. Territorial questions and arguments of power, obsolete though they are, still prevail over the essential demands of common welfare and justice.

Einstein then went on to talk about a specific case: the plight of his own people, the European Jews.

While in Europe territories are being distributed without any qualms about the wishes of the people concerned, the remainders of European Jewry, one-fifth of its pre-war population are again denied access to their haven in Palestine and left to hunger and cold and persisting hostility. There is no country, even today, that would be willing or be able to offer them a place where they could live in peace and security. And the fact that many of them are still kept in the degrading conditions of concentration camps by the Allies gives sufficient evidence of the shamefulness and hopelessness of the situation.

How to Build Courage to Act According to Our Own Convictions?

1. Be sure that you are convinced about what you are doing. The entire process starts and ends here. If you are fully convinced about something, you will be able to stand by it, whatever it takes.
2. Be prepared to face the consequences. Once you accept the consequences of your actions, it will be easy to act. Most of the time, we don't act because of fear of the consequences.
3. Know your own limitations. Don't stick your neck out when you know you won't be able to handle it. Don't bite off more than you can chew.
4. Fake it till you make it. Have confidence in yourself and your abilities. You can trick and train your mind by pretending to be strong.
5. Look at your intrinsic strengths and try building them. There are many qualities and virtues that are linked to the courage of one's convictions. Out of the following qualities, pick up your strengths: Consistency, patriotism,

dedication, genuineness, commitment, loyalty, honesty, devotedness, righteousness, sincerity, reliability, solidarity.

> *'Success is not final, failure is not fatal; it is the courage to continue that counts.'*
> —Winston Churchill

LESSONS FROM THE LIFE OF AN INNOVATIVE GENIUS

1. You must have a value system of your own. Keep reviewing it from time to time and listen to your heart.
2. Learn to speak your mind where it matters.
3. Be prepared to take risks for what you stand for, but you should know how far to go and understand your limitations.
4. If our actions are backed by our own values, we should not worry about what others think about them.

12

ADOPT THE PERSONA OF EINSTEIN

Develop a Charismatic Personality

'Science is not only a disciple of reason but, also, one of romance and passion.'
—Stephen Hawking

Overwhelming Popularity as a Scientist, Philosopher and Activist

While in school, we all came across names of some inventors and scientists. Those who studied science used the theories, discoveries and formulae of several scientists and can easily recall some of these names. For example, we heard about Avogadro's number, Boyle's and Charles's laws, studied Newton's laws of motion, Planck's constant and Rutherford Bohr's model of the atom, to name a few. As students, we did not have much exposure to the theories and discoveries of Einstein. Yet, each one of us has a perception of him as the greatest scientist, the most intelligent person, the father of physics and atomic science. There have been other giants of science like Sir Isaac Newton and Galileo Galilei in the past but Einstein is the most known, a household name across the world. Paul Dirac, a Nobel laureate, hailed the theory of general relativity as the greatest scientific discovery ever made.

Einstein's fame

In 1999, a poll conducted by *Physics World* magazine voted Einstein as the greatest physicist ever. He is the only scientist who is such a celebrity; whose name and fame matches popular film personalities like Marilyn Monroe, Brad Pitt and Tom Cruise. He gets more than 28 million hits on a Google search!

Earning big bucks even after his death

In 2008, Forbes's ranking of the highest-earning dead celebrities ranked Einstein fourth in the world, with Elvis Presley, cartoonist Charles Schulz and actor Heath Ledger ahead of him. Einstein was ahead of names like Marilyn Monroe and John Lennon. His average earnings per annum for the past several years has been around US$20 million. He has no heir and has bequeathed his entire intellectual property rights to the Hebrew University of Jerusalem.

Dead singers and writers earn royalty from their songs and books, but how does Einstein earn so much royalty? Anybody using his name and pictures has to pay royalty, and that earns him money. There are mugs, baby Einstein products, books, toys, educational e-products and DVDs, which earn huge royalties in his name.

How Did Einstein Become So Popular?

Einstein is also known as the engineer of the world and is popular amongst all age groups.

When he was asked as to what was it that fascinated people about him, he said, 'It is the mystery of not understanding my theories that fascinated people.' They looked up to him in awe as the ultimate scientist. His subjects were very complex, yet they interested everyone. For several thousand years, man desired to know about the limitations of the universe, its expanse, the galaxies and stars. Einstein talked about all of these; he also talked about the basic nature of matter, the invisible particles. He created the fourth dimension, talked about the speed of light, something people could never even imagine. His idea of converting a tiny mass of matter into an enormous amount of energy was like a fantasy. For the uninitiated, he was a fantasy scientist, a magician, a storyteller, a sorcerer, and for some he was an enigma.

At the same time, his theories appeared to be very simple. He answered basic questions like, 'Why is the sky blue?' It is because of the cumulative effect of the scattering of light by individual molecules in the atmosphere which he called 'critical opalescence'. His most famous equation is short yet relevant: $E=mc^2$, where E is energy and m is mass of matter and c, the speed of light. Most people know this as an extremely important equation of scientific discovery, but very few understand its meaning or impact. His research was on movement of particles or 'Brownian motion'. He also demonstrated a method to calculate Avogadro's number. He threw light on cosmos and cosmology. He researched on a number of subjects. There was, therefore, something about him to capture everyone's imagination.

The scientific community also respected him a lot. An equally important scientist, Neils Bohr, looked up to him with warmth and regard. Einstein was also very respectful and valued the work of other scientists in equal measure. In 1920, while he was studying Bohr's discoveries, he wrote to him: 'I am studying your great works and when I get stuck somewhere I look at your friendly face.' They both worked well as colleagues. Einstein was therefore popular within the scientific community because of his warmth and respect for everyone.

Different People, Different Perceptions

Though we all know Einstein today as a genius, he was considered an absolutely mediocre student during his childhood. He did not speak till he was three years old and had a funny pointy head, and his parents and relatives thought that there was something seriously wrong with him. He was perceived as insubordinate, lazy and disinterested in studies as well as other activities. He was very inquisitive and asked questions that his teachers were unable to answer. But then the school system was such that deviation from rote learning was neither encouraged nor prescribed.

Even during his polytechnic days, he found the teaching boring and rudimentary. So everyone wanted to know how a simple disinterested boy became the most celebrated scientist of the century. This was also one of the reasons why people were intrigued by him.

Even though he was a German Jew, he could manage to escape the clutches of Hitler and his Nazi cronies. He took refuge in America, where he was received with open arms. Meanwhile the Germans declared him an enemy of the state. They burnt his papers and books and ransacked his home. This kind of treatment by the Germans further raised his esteem in the eyes of the world.

'Personality is the glitter that sends your little gleam across the footlights and the orchestra pit into that big black space where the audience is.'

—Mae West

Different people define charisma differently. For some it is a rare personal quality that helps an individual to influence others. Sometimes it is related to personal magnetism or simply overwhelming charm.

History is replete with examples of charisma and great personalities from almost all walks of life. Hitler, Churchill, John F. Kennedy and Indira Gandhi as political leaders could cast their spell on millions. The Beatles, ABBA and Elvis Presley mesmerized millions with their music. Peter O'Toole, Richard Burton, Richard Harris, Al Pacino, Amitabh Bachchan and Morgan Freeman swayed the world with their acting skills.

Is It Only Theatrics?

Many people feel that dressing up, gestures, body language and moving around on the stage is all you require to develop a great persona. While these things help a lot, there are more subtle things that could help build a charismatic personality. In fact, charisma is a heady mix of many qualities. Wit, for instance, contributed to a great extent. Those who are witty and humorous are charming. People are attracted to them. To be a great persona, you need to have at least one very strong trait and along with that, a string of other supporting elements.

For instance, in the case of Adolf Hitler, his primary charisma lay in his oratory skills. To support this he dressed differently, largely stage-managed his speeches and created impactful props like a colourful flag with a swastika and an eagle to create shock and awe.

In the case of Barack Obama, it is his oratory, clarity of thought and speech which is his primary strength. Supporting this is his in-depth homework, knowledge and great sense of timing and response. Amitabh Bachchan primarily has a very impactful voice and great acting skills. He is backed by strong dialogues, great tailor-made scripts and a lanky, tall frame.

Churchill displayed unbeatable confidence, a gruff voice and well-articulated speeches. He was plump, not great to look at, but he was always sure of himself and thus inspired confidence in his team—confidence to win at all costs.

For The Beatles, it was their great new music that made them a phenomenon. It was their primary strength. Their stylish haircuts, long side-burns and new dancing style added to their charm. I feel that having a charismatic personality is a package deal. If you have some primary strengths you can easily build a few secondary strengths around these and highlight your charisma.

In case of Einstein, his primary strengths were his high level of intelligence, great research and deep understanding of his subject. Wit, humour, the courage to speak his mind, dressing up casually and a 'couldn't-care-less' attitude became his secondary supportive strengths.

Personality Is Not Black and White

Having a charismatic personality is not something which you either have or you don't. It is not completely black and white. Some people radiate more charisma than others. It is like a light bulb with a dimmer switch—you can adjust it yourself. The 'filament' of the bulb is like your primary strength—you must have a filament, otherwise the bulb will not even light up.

Secondary strength can be compared to the amount of electric energy one allows to flow in the filament through an additional diversionary circuit. Therefore, have a primary filament by identifying what you are best at and then build a secondary circuit, which enhances the primary and makes the bulb light up to the maximum capacity.

> *'But charisma only wins people's attention. Once you have their attention, you have to have something to tell them.'*
> —Daniel Quinn

How to Develop a Great Persona

Be yourself

This is the most important piece of advice. Don't put up a false front. You will get caught in no time. Be what you are and let people know your strengths as well as weaknesses. You must appear to be truthful as much as you actually are. This will establish trust between you and your audience.

Remain comfortable and don't worry about the results

The audience can gauge you and your depth easily. If you are nervous, people will find you out. Your physical presence affects your believability. Great actors are known to have 'screen presence', which means to be in a commanding position during every shot.

Use humour and emotions

If you speak from your heart, you will speak sincerely. What you speak is important, but it is more important to know how to speak. An emotional approach touches people's hearts and humour connects you to your audience.

Don't have a one-way-street approach

Talking to people without listening to them or not having a dialogue with them can be very boring for your audience. To keep them engaged, you must take up questions frequently. Involve your audience and let them participate too.

Have a commanding stance

Your body language should be such that people find you confident and self-assured.

Master your subject

Be fully prepared and have complete knowledge of your subject. This is also one of the most important factors for a charismatic personality.

'Charm is more than beauty.'
—Yiddish Proverb

LESSONS FROM THE LIFE OF AN INNOVATIVE GENIUS

1. Charisma is not necessarily an innate quality. It can be gradually cultivated. A charismatic personality can therefore be built over a period of time.
2. You must have one or more major strengths as your primary qualities around which you can develop your personality. This could be oratory, the ability to sing or even excellent domain knowledge of your specialization.
3. Identify your secondary strengths, which can help augment your primary capabilities. This could be your ability to network with people, a good dressing sense or self-confidence.
4. Combine your primary strengths with your secondary strengths to develop a great persona. And then keep working on it consistently.

EPILOGUE

The Twenty-seventh Alphabet

Albert Einstein, without doubt, is the greatest scientist of the last century. This book has covered almost every facet of this genius, which would be enough to inspire any young or mature mind. I have touched upon not only his scientific prowess but also his other interests and endeavours to add value to the world he lived in.

His discoveries and theories were not clearly understood by many scientists and intellectuals and definitely not by ordinary people. Yet, he became, and still is, a household name—'Einstein' being synonymous to 'intelligence'. He could sit and dine with kings and presidents and yet spend time with commoners with equal ease. He did what he thought was right and spoke his heart. Even more than hundred years after his great discoveries in 1905, he is still a hero, ever fresh in the minds of people across the world. He was a thinker, philosopher, an activist, a scientist at heart and a childlike inventor.

He solved the riddles of an ordinary mind—how can mass be converted to energy? Why does the sky look blue? Does our universe end at any point, and is it static or expanding? He answered it all. His theory of relativity and especially his explanation of the atom and subatomic particles laid the foundation for modern solid-state physics and electronics, without which we cannot imagine our lives. He gave a different meaning to the speed of light and created the shortest yet most powerful equation: $E=mc^2$.

Simplicity was at the core of his existence, his approach to life, work and even day-to-day living. While he was delivering a lecture, he said that the laws of physics should be simple. When a person from the audience said, 'What if they are not simple?' Einstein retorted, 'Then I will not be interested in them.' His general theory of relativity was viewed by scientists as the most simple and beautiful theory ever formulated. The legend himself said that hardly anyone who had truly understood his relativity theory would be able to escape the charm of this fascinating hypothesis. It was one man's view on how the universe ought to be and, amazingly, the universe turned out exactly as he described it. The mathematics of it, though complex, could explain the phenomenon of black holes. He simply plucked his ideas from the universe or Brahmand. His theories gave us the most important existential truth: 'A complete harmonious account of existence.'

His explanations were simple and he could articulate the most complex things in a very simple manner. It was not surprising that he once said: 'If a mouse looks at the universe, will the universe look different or will it change its status?'

His personal life was uncluttered and simple. He had no qualms about his clothes, hair, or daily needs. He was in a state of ecstasy while he worked and on cloud nine when he played his violin.

He was a political and social activist, a philanthropist and, above all, a man of high thinking and simple living. Students, colleagues and even children could easily approach him. He was unassuming in the real sense. Wit and humour were in his blood. Perhaps he is the only scientist till date who has coined so many quotes—one better than the other on almost every subject. He has intelligently commented on almost all the issues of his time as well as those that he could foresee in the future.

Albert Einstein collaborated with great intellectuals of his time professionally and also played the violin in an orchestra with people like Max Planck, who were giants in their own fields of research. Dead singers and celebrities earn royalties from their work and Einstein earns millions of dollars every year, even sixty years after his death, by just lending his name. He was a celebrity while he lived and will remain a legend till eternity.

In his capacity as a responsible citizen, Einstein always opposed the war which, to his mind, was senseless killing of humans. He opposed the production of nuclear weapons as he realized the havoc that weapons of the future could cause if further research was not halted in time. He could foresee that even more destructive weapons would be produced than what he had witnessed during the bombings of Nagasaki and Hiroshima in August 1945. He was so accurate in his prediction that just six years after his death, the USSR, in 1961, tested their most powerful nuclear bomb, Tsar Bomba, which had a yield of more than 50 megatons, equivalent to 50 million tons of TNT. This was about 1,600 times the combined power of the bombs that destroyed Hiroshima and Nagasaki, and ten times the combined power of all the conventional explosives used in World War II, in the six-year war across the world! It started the era of hydrogen bombs and ushered in the Cold War between America and Russia. Today, 100-megaton weapons are a reality.

Einstein redefined God and separated Him from religion. He spoke his mind and never bothered to look over his shoulder. He was a staunch Jew and gave almost all his belongings and royalties for building knowledge, for universities and libraries. He didn't really possess anything much personally. He existed as if he was born to create.

He redefined life, did not fear death and lived life on his own terms. As a boy, he was born with a swollen misshapen head, was overweight at birth and had an unusually angular back to his head. When faced with an internal rupture in the abdominal area, he refused surgery. He did not want to live an inactive life and therefore said, 'I want to go when I want. It is tasteless to prolong life artificially. I have done my share, it is time to go and I will do it elegantly.'

As I come to the end of this book and write the last few lines, I have become increasingly aware that an effective individual sometimes needs to define his own rules—his own lexicon. Einstein showed the entire world (especially the scientific community) that he defined his own operational grammar and created a twenty-seventh alphabet of his own—not available in any dictionary, out of the box. He ceased to be a part of the crowd and stood out as an individual. Though born with an actual swollen head, he never showed off. Born to be a genius, he lived like a maverick.

In today's chaotic world of business and politics, there could be no one formula for success than this—define your own lexicon and create that twenty-seventh alphabet that fits into your prose of success.